THE SYRINGE LOOMED CLOSER

"Damn it!" Remo thought as the needle jammed into his shoulder. "It might be poison." Suddenly his head began to throb violently.

"Biggest dose yet," said the blond man to his companion.

Remo's head was splitting. He tried to rise but felt something brush against his face. Something made of cloth. He felt his arms being pulled across his body. A straitjacket!

Then he landed hard on the sofa, and he heard the door lock shut behind the two men. The pain behind his eyes was blinding. His mouth was dry, and a chill racked his body. He had to get out!

He strained to roll over onto his back. Each movement brought a new flash of pain to his head. The throbbing was spreading now from behind his eyes into the center of his skull, deep into his brain. He could feel his strength draining away. He tried to ignore the pain, but it was overpowering. What had they dosed him with?

Could it be the aging drug?

THE DESTROYER SERIES:

#1   CREATED, THE DESTROYER
#2   DEATH CHECK
#3   CHINESE PUZZLE
#4   MAFIA FIX
#5   DR. QUAKE
#6   DEATH THERAPY
#7   UNION BUST
#8   SUMMIT CHASE
#9   MURDER'S SHIELD
#10   TERROR SQUAD
#11   KILL OR CURE
#12   SLAVE SAFARI
#13   ACID ROCK
#14   JUDGMENT DAY
#15   MURDER WARD
#16   OIL SLICK
#17   LAST WAR DANCE
#18   FUNNY MONEY
#19   HOLY TERROR
#20   ASSASSIN'S PLAY-OFF
#21   DEADLY SEEDS
#22   BRAIN DRAIN
#23   CHILD'S PLAY
#24   KING'S CURSE
#25   SWEET DREAMS
#26   IN ENEMY HANDS
#27   THE LAST TEMPLE
#28   SHIP OF DEATH
#29   THE FINAL DEATH
#30   MUGGER BLOOD
#31   THE HEAD MEN
#32   KILLER CHROMOSOMES
#33   VOODOO DIE
#34   CHAINED REACTION
#35   LAST CALL
#36   POWER PLAY
#37   BOTTOM LINE

THE DESTROYER
MURDER WARD

by

Richard Sapir and Warren Murphy

PINNACLE BOOKS • LOS ANGELES

THE DESTROYER: MURDER WARD

An original Pinnacle Books edition, published for the
first time anywhere.

ISBN: 0-523-40289-9

First printing, April 1974
Second printing, February 1977
Third printing, April 1978
Fourth printing, May 1979
Fifth printing, September 1979

Printed in the United States of America

PINNACLE BOOKS, INC.
2029 Century Park East
Los Angeles, California 90067

For Rita, who sits on a stool; David, who should sit at his typewriter; Etta, who sits away from the table; and Mimi, who doesn't sit very much at all . . .

CHAPTER ONE

Dr. Daniel Demmet was a true professional. When he decided it was time to kill his patient, he first made sure that the critical body functions were doing well. He checked the electrocardiogram screen, as he had been checking it since the patient had been wheeled into the operating room of the Robler Clinic, one of the finer hospitals just outside of Baltimore. Dr. Demmet sat on a stool behind the patient's head, from which point, as a modern anesthesiologist, he could best supervise and protect the patient's hold on life. The surgeon, working a few feet from him, was too busy rearranging the body with instruments to worry about his life. The surgeon worked on the appendix; the anesthesiologist worked on the patient.

The screen showed normal sinus rhythm, a sharp beeping line across the screen, which caught the electrical impulses from the heart. At the first stage of trouble, the wave would become ectopic, indicating cardiac malfunction.

On the screen, death was a smooth flowing line, with little hills; life was sharp and discordant. What Dr. Demmet continuously looked at was the line that guaranteed life. Perfect. A perfect sinus rhythm. The low hill, the deep valley, the high peak, another valley, and then the pattern all over again. All this in a beep. Life.

Perfect. But then, why shouldn't it be? The patient was healthy, and Dr. Demmet had done his job well, in the best tradition of modern, balanced anesthesia. Gone were the days when good doctors would knock out a patient with a single massive dose of a potentially lethal chemical, with the inevitable residual toxicity that left the recovering patient nauseated, uncomfortable, and, sometimes, in pain.

Now, anesthesia is a symphony. Demmet had given the patient, a healthy, forty-five-year-old male, an initial injection of sodium pentothol, which put him quickly to sleep. The opening note.

Then oxygen through the anesthesia machine to assure good breathing. Intravenously, the succinylcholine, which relaxed the body muscles and made way for the endotracheal intubation, affording Dr. Demmet greater control over the patient's breathing. Then, through the anesthesia machine, nitrous oxide, a further nerve depressant. And finally halothane. Very carefully with the halothane, for this was the basic anesthetic of the operation.

It was also what was going to kill the patient.

Intravenously, Dr. Demmet administered a small amount of curare to relax the stomach muscles, making the appendectomy that much easier for the surgeon to perform. The electrodes of the electrocardiograph were attached to both arms and a leg. There was a constant intravenous flow of 5 percent dextrose. Dr. Demmet felt for the pulse, checked the blood pressure, listened to the heartbeat through a stethoscope, which was not of course as accurate as the electrocardiogram but still a good backup check. Then he proceeded to kill the patient.

He also did something that never appears in television dramas or great romances about hospitals but that is not at all uncommon in real operating rooms.

2

He passed gas. Sitting on high stools for several hours, under great tension and with great need for concentration, anesthesiologists help make operating rooms smell more like lavatories than like Marcus Welby's office. This is reality. No one ever comments, because everyone is too busy to notice.

Dr. Demmet increased the level of halothane. He did not do it with a jolt. Everything was precise. He watched the screen. Normal sinus rhythm. He increased the halothane. The ectopic response came with a flutter. Gone were the high discordant peaks. More halothane, and he watched the ectopic leveling become bigeminal—two small beeps. A more even pattern on the EKG. Ordinarily, this pattern on the screen would have set a flurry of emergency measures into motion, but it took the anesthesiologist to alert the team. Instead, Dr. Demmet watched the screen. Still bigeminal. The pulse lowered, blood pressure lowered, heartbeat weak and struggling. The patient needed no more halothane.

In three minutes and forty-five seconds by Demmet's watch, the screen showed a smooth, even-flowing, up-and-down line. Dr. Demmet relaxed. For the first time since the operation began, he felt the hardness of the stool. He watched the surgeon work, watched the nurse count the sponges and make sure that everything brought to the operating table remained there, not inside the patient. A sponge or a clamp left inside a patient could mean a malpractice suit, even though a sponge might not do much harm. The supervising nurse's real job was the first step in the professional web that made it almost impossible for a doctor to lose a malpractice suit. Naturally, the patient's bill showed the cost of the nurse's services.

Dr. Demmet waited another two minutes and then turned off the halothane, reduced the nitrous oxide, folded his arms, and watched the peaceful, level hills of death.

When the surgeon looked up, Demmet shook his head. "I'm sorry. We've lost him," he said.

The announcement snapped everyone's head toward the EKG screen, where the beeping dot painted the landscape of oblivion.

The surgeon glared angrily at Demmet. He would complain later that Dr. Demmet should have let him know that the patient was in trouble. And Demmet would inform the surgeon that he had done everything possible to save the patient and that if the surgeon had any complaints, he should go see Ms. Hahl, the assistant administrator of the hospital.

Now Dr. Demmet sat on the high stool, the stethoscope hanging from his neck, his ears blissfully free of any foreign objects, and watched the surgeon complete the operation down to the last suture. If no one left a sponge inside, and the nurse would see to that, then the operation was safely over, and no subsequent autopsy was ever going to reveal that the surgeon was at fault. When the surgeon left, sullenly and silently, Demmet rose from the stool, stretched his muscles and went out to break the tragic news to the next of kin. He had a reputation at the Robler Clinic of being the best at breaking this sort of news.

It is a fact of hospital life that doctors instinctively avoid dying patients and spend more time with those who are going to get well. Even now, across the nation, doctors are just beginning to study their own attitudes toward the dying, something that they have instinctively avoided for centuries, though the rest of the populace believes that they are not uncomfortable with death. Doctors are supposed to be men of great compassion, courage, and knowledge. But it is only now being admitted that a doctor often avoids telling

4

a patient his illness is terminal, not for the patient's benefit but for his own.

Demmet, unlike his colleagues, had no such troubles. He whisked off his mask, examined his cool aquiline face for any resurgence of pimples, touched up his just-graying sandy-blond hair with his fingertips, removed his surgical gown, and went to the administrative offices to make the usual report for this special sort of operation.

"What was it this time? Heart failure?" asked a graceful young woman with dark red hair and cool brown eyes. She was Kathy Hahl, assistant administrator of the hospital and director of hospital development, another term for chief fund raiser.

"Yeah. Heart failure will do," said Demmet. "You know, the sand wedge, the damned sand wedge, is a disaster off the fairway."

"Not if you use it right. If you use it right, it's like a scalpel. Puts the ball just where you want it if you use it right," said Ms. Hahl.

"If you can play six hours a day every day," said Demmet testily.

"You get *your* game a day if you want it."

"Not if I can't schedule these operations but have to take them mid-day, afternoons. Morning or late afternoon are too cold for golf these days."

"A lot of doctors work twenty-four hours in a row sometimes, even come in in the wee hours. It's not a profession conducive to rest, Dan."

"If I wanted an easy life, I wouldn't have to be going down to that waiting room now to tell the widow What's-her-name that her husband didn't survive an appendectomy. Really, the way you set things up, I'm going to have to work up a routine for terminal head cold."

"Her name's Nancy Boulder. Mrs. Nancy Boulder.

Her husband's name was John. John Boulder. He was with the Internal Revenue Service."

"We seem to be getting a few Internal Revenue specials nowadays. Some sort of trend?" Demmet asked.

"Not your worry, Dan."

"Boulder. John Boulder," Demmet repeated. "If I keep on getting these specials, I'll never break eighty."

"If the sand wedge doesn't work for you, try running the ball up to the green. You can use a three iron like a heavy putter," said Kathy Hahl.

Demmet stared at a large red arrow painted on a sign that said $20 million advancement goal. The arrow was almost reaching the top of the black line that marked progress.

"But the wedge looks so nice popping up on the green and stopping."

"Do you want form or score?"

"I want both."

"So do we all, Dan. Give the widow Boulder your regrets, and I'll meet you at the club."

"I'd like three strokes a side."

"Your handicap is big enough already."

"I'll use my pitching wedge, my old pitching wedge. Three strokes a side," Demmet said.

"Two," said Kathy Hahl, smiling the special smile that made men aware of their own heartbeat.

"You're a cruel, hard, ungiving person," said Dr. Demmet.

"Never forget that, Dan," said Kathy Hahl.

When Dr. Demmet told the head nurse he wished to see a Mrs. Nancy Boulder who was in the waiting room, the nurse asked, "Another one?"

"Are you keeping score?" asked Dr. Demmet stern-

6

ly. The nurse had violated professional decorum, and she knew it.

"No, doctor. My apologies."

"Accepted," said Dr. Demmet.

Nancy Boulder was in the waiting room, explaining to an elderly gentleman that he really had no cause for worry, when she heard a nurse call her name. She excused herself momentarily from the man, who was fingering a small brown paper bag, and quietly told the nurse she would be with her in a minute.

"I think it's important," said the nurse.

"That man is important, too," said Nancy Boulder. "He's in agony. His wife is having a hysterectomy and . . ."

"A hysterectomy is nothing to worry about."

"That's not the point," said Nancy Boulder. "He thinks so, and he's terrified. I just can't leave him here. Give me a minute, please."

The nurse sighed in resignation, and Nancy Boulder went back to the man, who, in his anxiety, hardly heard her words. But she tried.

"Listen. I know it's very important to you and your wife. It is to the hospital, too. But just because it's important doesn't mean it's dangerous. They do these operations because they are safe."

The man nodded dully.

"I don't know what to say to you, sir, but you're going to look back on this someday and laugh," said Nancy Boulder, giving him a big, hopeful smile. He saw the smile and like so many others who knew her, could not resist its warmth and openness. He smiled back briefly.

Well, at least he had a brief respite, thought Nancy Boulder. It was a nice thing about people that they responded to warmth. She tried to explain this to the nurse, but the nurse did not seem to understand. She just asked Mrs. Boulder to follow her please.

"You know, it's funny how superstitions linger. Even John had a premonition," Nancy said to the nurse. "He was in pain. But when the doctor told us it was appendicitis, I stopped worrying. An appendectomy is the simplest operation in the world, isn't it?"

"Well," said the nurse. "No operation is really simple."

There was something in her tone that made Mrs. Boulder's hands tighten. She tried to remain calm. All the nurse had said was that no operation was simple. That was all.

Mrs. Boulder's dark, middle-aged face suddenly showed the lines normally hidden by her ever-present smile. The happy brown eyes became dull with a gnawing terror and her brisk gait became a forced trudge. She held her pocketbook in front of her chest like a shield. All the nurse had said was that no operation was simple. So why should she worry?

"Everything worked out all right, didn't it?" asked Mrs. Boulder. "I mean, John is all right, isn't he? Tell me he's all right!"

"The doctor will explain everything," said the nurse.

"I mean he's all right. He's all right, isn't he? John's all right." Mrs. Boulder's voice rose, loud and tense. She grasped the nurse by an arm. "Tell me John's all right. Tell me he's all right."

"Your husband was not my patient."

"Was? Was?"

"He is not my patient. *Is*," said the nurse and freed her arm with a fast snap of the elbow.

"Oh, thank God," said Mrs. Boulder. "Thank merciful God."

8

The nurse, beyond an arm's distance, led Mrs. Boulder down the corridor to a frosted glass door that read, "Anesthesiology. Dr. Daniel Demmet, Chief."

"The doctor is waiting for you," said the nurse, knocking twice on the door. Before Mrs. Boulder could say thank you for showing her the way to the doctor's office, the nurse was gone, walking very quickly down the hall as if on an urgent matter. If Mrs. Boulder had not had as much faith in hospitals as she did, she would have sworn it was flight.

Dr. Demmet heard the knock and put his sand wedge into a closet. He had been chipping peanuts from the wall-to-wall dull gray carpeting to the back of a worn leather chair. If he could chip a peanut off a carpet with a sand wedge, why couldn't he do it with a golf ball close to the green?

This was the problem, then, that faced him as the distraught woman entered. He knew immediately that the nurse had let on. He saw Mrs. What's-her-name, clutching her pocketbook, knuckles white. Her jaw quivered.

"Will you sit down please?" said Dr. Demmet, motioning to the green leather chair near his desk. He whisked away the peanuts with a swipe of his left hand.

"Thank you," said Mrs. Boulder. "Everything is all right, isn't it?"

Dr. Demmet's face was somber. He lowered his eyes momentarily, circled the desk and sat down, even though he knew he must rise again in a moment. He made a cathedral arch of his fingers before him, nails immaculately white, hands scrubbed clean, clean to the redness of the palms and knuckles.

Dr. Demmet stared mournfully at the hands. Mrs. Boulder trembled.

"We did everything we could for Jim," said Dr. Demmet.

"John," corrected Mrs. Boulder weakly.

"We did everything we could for John. There were complications."

"No," cried Mrs. Boulder.

"The heart gave out. The appendectomy was perfect. Perfect. It was the heart."

"No. Not John. Not John. No!" cried Mrs. Boulder, and then the tears came in overwhelming grief.

"We took every precaution," said Dr. Demmet. He let the first rush of grief run itself out before he rose from his seat, placed a comforting arm around the widow, helped her to her feet, and out the door to the first nurse they encountered in the hallway, giving explicit instructions that everything that was possible should be done for this woman. He ordered a mild sedative.

"What is her name, doctor?" asked the nurse.

"She'll give it to you," said Dr. Demmet.

By the time he reached the Fair Oaks Country Club outside Baltimore, he knew what he must do. He could delay it no longer. He was only deceiving himself if he thought he could, and he was not one to encourage self-deception.

"I've got to give that funny knuckle club a chance," Dr. Demmet told the golf pro. "I've tried the sand wedge, considered going back to running a three iron onto the green, but I've got to give your club a chance."

"It doesn't look pretty, Dr. Demmet, but it certainly gets the ball up to the hole from anywhere near the apron," said the pro.

"I suppose so," said Dr. Demmet sadly, and this time the mournful tone was sincere.

10

Mrs. Boulder woke up at three in the morning in her bedroom, saw that her husband's bed had not been slept in, and realized he would not be coming home. She had told the children the night before, and they had cried. She had spoken with the funeral people and paid more than she could afford, not really caring all that much and almost welcoming the assault of the high expenses. She had told John's brother, who would notify the rest of the family, and she had received a multitude of sympathy calls. But it was in the morning that she realized in her body and in her senses, finally understood, and began to accept that John would not be coming home again. It was then that the grief came, full and deep and unremitting.

She wanted to share the grief with him as she had shared everything else with him since they were married after his graduation from the University of Maryland. It was too much pain for her to bear alone, and she did not know how to pray.

So she began to pack his things, trying to separate what her son might want from what John's brother might want from what the Salvation Army might want. In the basement, she taped his cross-country skis together, packed his squash rackets, and wondered why he had never thrown out his old jogging sneakers. She left his scuba tanks in the corner because they were too heavy to lift.

And when she looked back at all those pairs of jogging sneakers, tattered testimony of the three miles he had run every day of their marriage, except during the honeymoon, it came to her with a jarring shock.

"Heart gave out. No way. No way. No way."

John did not smoke, rarely drank, exercised daily,

watched his diet, and no one in his family had ever suffered heart disease.

"No way," she said again, and she was suddenly very excited as though by establishing this fact conclusively, it would in some way bring him back.

She forced herself to wait until nine-thirty in the morning before phoning the family physician. The doctor's receptionist-nurse answered, and she made an appointment for that day. She only needed five minutes, she said.

Actually, she needed less.

"John's heart was in good shape, wasn't it, doctor?" she asked before he could offer his sympathy.

"Well, yes. For a man of his age, his heart was functioning well. He took care of himself properly."

"Should his heart have failed on the operating table?"

"Well, Mrs. Boulder, an operation puts an incredible strain on the body."

"Should it have failed?"

"Robler has some of the finest surgical teams in the country, Mrs. Boulder. Many of the nation's highest officials go there. If there were any way for them to save your husband . . ."

"He shouldn't have died of a heart failure, should he, doctor? Tell me. You're our family physician."

"Mrs. Boulder, I sent my own daughter to the Robler Clinic."

"But John shouldn't have died of heart failure in his condition at his age, should he?"

"There are many things in medicine that we can't explain," he said. But Mrs. Boulder wasn't listening to him; she was already composing her letter to the American Medical Association and the medical societies. By afternoon she was outlining her strategy to the family lawyer. He was more blunt than the family doctor.

"Save your money, Mrs. Boulder. The only way we can get the Robler people for malpractice is to get another physician to testify against them."

"Well, let's do that."

"It's a fine strategy, Mrs. Boulder. But it won't work."

"Why not?" she asked, her voice sharp and angry.

"Because if your own family physician wouldn't back you up in private, what do you expect from some impartial doctor in the courtroom? Doctors don't testify against doctors. That's not in the Hippocratic oath, but it's one rule doctors follow faithfully."

"You mean doctors can kill patients and get away with it?"

"I mean sometimes they don't perform well, or even properly, and there's nothing anyone can do about it."

"I read of a doctor out west who was convicted of malpractice just last . . . last . . . last year, I think it was."

"That's right. You read of it. When a doctor is convicted of malpractice, it's news. And I believe that doctor was an oddball who had made waves and was fighting the medical societies. Did you read about the auto accident in Phoenix where the driver was found guilty of careless driving and reckless endangerment?"

"No, I don't think I did."

"Neither did I. That's because people are regularly convicted of careless driving. Policemen testify. For doctors, there are no policemen."

"But there are medical boards, laws, the American Medical Association."

"The AMA? That's like asking the National Association of Manufacturers to investigate excessive profits. Mrs. Boulder, I'm your friend, and I was John's friend.

13

And as your friend and as a good lawyer, which I am, I'm going to give you some excellent professional advice. And by the way, I'm going to charge you for it, so you'd better listen to me. To bring a malpractice suit against the Robler Clinic or Dr. Demmet is a waste of your time and your money and your emotions. I won't let you do it because you can't win."

"What about an autopsy?"

"We can get one."

"Well, won't that prove our case?"

"It will probably prove Robler's case."

"The coroners are part of the club, too? Is that what you're saying?"

"It's not what I'm saying. They're not. But doctors, like everyone else, learn to cover themselves properly. If they say heart failure was the cause of death, then that's just what the coroner is going to find. A medical career is worth more than a million dollars. Doctors don't risk that lightly. Now, I will do something else. If you promise not to pursue this, Mrs. Boulder, I'll forget the bill for this appointment. I'm sorry. I grieve with you, and if there were some way we could bring John back, even on the longest chance, or make amends for his death, I would go with you on this thing despite the odds. But there's nothing we can do. I'm sorry."

"We'll see," said Mrs. Boulder, who was not thanking people for their services anymore.

Her letters were answered politely, giving the impression that the correspondents had looked into the matter. But when she reread them and analyzed each sentence carefully, she realized that all the authorities had said was how wonderful the profession of medicine was and how thorough doctors were in their concern.

14

And there she finally let the matter drop. The only time she ever saw Dr. Demmet's name again was in the sports pages when he won the low gross in the Fair Oaks Scotch Foursome winter tournament.

CHAPTER TWO

His name was Remo and the Bay winds out of the Pacific whipped at him with all the fury gathered over the vast stretch of ocean. The Golden Gate spun out before him to Marin County, the gateway to the northwest. Behind him was San Francisco and going east, the rest of America.

He stood on the guardrail, where four hundred and ninety-nine others had plunged to their deaths in suicides marking otherwise insignificant lives.

The man was about six feet tall, normal in build. Only extra-thick wrists suggested he might be more than just an ordinary man, but there was nothing in the wrists to suggest that he could be standing there with the soles of his bare feet just touching the round railing of the bridge.

For one thing, Volkswagens crossing the bridge in the pre-dawn darkness tended to shift as the cross-gusts buffeted them. For another, his dark pants and dark shirt whipped like flags in a hurricane. And for another, he stood upright, very casual as if doing nothing more enervating than contemplating a change of television channel in his living room.

He smelled the salt Pacific breeze and felt the

December cold that kept car windows closed and left many rear windows clouded with steam.

The cold he handled simply, by letting his body become one with it, as he was taught. The wind he handled another way. It was not that his body fought the wind; it was that his body became stronger than the wind by becoming part of the bridge, connected by his very thoughts to the support driven deep into the bedrock that bordered the Bay.

"Are you waiting for applause?" came the squeaky Oriental voice from behind him. "Or are you about to make a great production of a simple exercise?"

"Thank you for distracting me. I really needed a distraction. If there's one thing I needed standing two hundred feet above open water with a winter wind whipping at me, it's a distraction," said Remo, turning around to the wispy Oriental in a dark black kimono, whose strands of white hair flew in the wind like vagrant silk threads, but who stood just as securely on the pedestrian walk as Remo did on the railing.

"If your mind is a slave to every noise, do not blame the noise for your subservience," said Chiun, the Master of Sinanju. "It is not a master that makes a slave, but a slave who makes those about him a master."

"Thank you for a very merry Christmas, Little Father."

"If your heart remains with a white man's holiday, then perhaps I should stand on that bar with you lest you fall, for truly, not even the House of Sinanju can overcome treasured bad habits."

"Well, I'm not going ga-ga over the Feast of the Pig."

"It is not called the Feast of the Pig," said Chiun. "It is a day when those who feel obligated to someone

17

who has given them much wisdom return some small little offering of thanksgiving."

"You're not getting Barbra Streisand," Remo said. "We don't give women like that around here."

"She would be good for bearing children. And seeing your shoddiness of performance, the House of Sinanju needs another male."

"She's not Korean, Little Father. She's as white as I am."

"For beauty, one makes an exception. The blood of Sinanju should overcome any inadequacies. And then I would get a pupil without learned bad habits and arrogance and talkativeness. Even the greatest of artists has difficulty molding hardened clay."

Remo turned back to the cold wind. He knew its sound was there but he did not hear it. He knew the cold was there but he did not feel it. He knew the bridge was beneath him and around him but he did not sense it. He was moving along a thin bar at an outside angle above dark waters and his thoughts and feelings were the center of his balance. He could run for days like this, he felt, and though he was aware of the lights of cars moving at him and beside him, they were not in his world. His world was passing them faster and faster and as his world approached the far side of the bridge, he reversed it in a spin that stopped not with his feet because his bones could not support that sort of jarring pressure, but with the very stopping of his world. And then he was moving back toward Chiun, the Master of Sinanju.

It had all started so simply a decade before with exercises that caused pain that he had never known his body could endure. But then the pain became different and the exercises that were at first difficult became easy, until his body knew what to do from

18

distant memory and his mind moved on to other things.

It was more than a change in the quality of his skills; it was a change of his very nervous system and his being. And if he had been truthful with Chiun, he would have admitted that most of his loneliness at Christmastime had left years before and he was now in his soul more a descendant of Sinanju, that tiny village in North Korea which had through the centuries produced assassins for the kings and emperors whose gold supported the rocky village where nothing seemed to grow.

Remo was the first Caucasian to be taught the secrets of Sinanju. For in hiring himself to "Upstairs," Chiun had agreed to train, instead of perform, and Chiun once admitted that he had given Remo more than what he called "the little tricks" of kung fu, aikido, and tae kwan do. He had given Remo the source of them all—Sinanju. And Upstairs had its white assassin who could move freely in a white society. Neat.

Remo's world moved back to Chiun, standing almost invisible on the walkway, and then Remo stopped, still motionless, still in perfect harmony with the deep-sunk bridge supports.

"You may begin," said Chiun.

"Begin? I've finished, Little Father."

"Did you really? I was not watching. I was thinking about my home across the waters. In the cold mornings, I think of Sinanju. I think of how there would be a gift waiting for me if I were home. I do not know what the gift would look like, or if she would be as gracious as the singer of songs, but it is not the size of the breast or hip, but the thought that counts. Oh, if I were but home."

"I can't give you a human being, Little Father."

"Who am I to expect a little nothing of a remembrance from one who has received so much from me?"

"If you want something warm, I'll get you a cow," said Remo.

"I already have a cow. He talks back to me," said Chiun, and Remo heard that cackle that indicated this saying would be coming back at him for several days. Along with the cackle.

"I have a cow already. He talks back to me," Chiun repeated. As much to get away from the tinkly laugh as anything else, Remo ran the Golden Gate again. This time he heard voices yelling, intruding into his moving world.

"That's him. Stop him. My God. He's going sideways. I don't believe it. Look at how fast he's going. He's going to jump. There. That guy on the bridge. Stop him."

When he returned to Chiun, he received a nod of recognition and hopped down from the railing.

"In Persia, the shah would have given a Master of Sinanju his own daughter. In Rome, the emperor once made an offering of a captured queen. In the great Selucid empire, ah, the great Selucid empire, they knew truly how to treat a Master of Sinanju. In Africa, the Loni* showed before your very eyes the proper respect paid to a Master of Sinanju. But in America, in America, I get a cow. A cow who talks back to me."

"Fish again for the meal, Little Father," said Remo, referring to the day meal that was several hours away, but might change the subject.

"If the fish does not talk back to me," said Chiun. "Heh, heh, heh."

A patrol car, its bubble light flashing, dashed past them toward the other end of the Golden Gate Bridge.

*See Destroyer #12, *Slave Safari.*

"I attracted some attention back there, Little Father."

"Clumsiness always wins an audience. True perfection is a quiet, hidden thing."

"Thank you once again, Little Father, for a merry Christmas."

When they returned to the Marina apartment overlooking the Bay that Upstairs had rented for them during this rest period, Remo found one of the shrubs in the front yard had been uprooted and was sitting in the middle of the rug, scattering dirt around the carpeting. On the branches of the shrub hung two punctured tennis balls, a golf ball popped open with incredible pressure and a slice of an apple. A bare yellow anti-bug light topped it all.

Chiun smiled. "For you. For your remembered customs."

"What is it, Little Father?"

"I made it for you. Since you cannot overcome your past, you might as well enjoy some of it."

Remo pointed to the cluttered bush.

"What is that thing?"

"Do not make witticisms with me. It is a Christmas tree. For your enjoyment."

"That's not a Christmas tree, Little Father. A Christmas tree is a pine tree and the decorations are made of glass and the lights are colored and . . ."

"It looks like a Christmas tree to me," said Chiun. "It looks just like a Christmas tree to me. It is green. It has things hanging on it. It has lights. It is a Christmas tree. I see no difference between that tree and the ones in the stores, except that I improved the form somewhat."

"Take my word for it. If you were an American, you would see it's not a Christmas tree."

"If I were an American, you would still be a fattened

senseless glob shooting guns at people, dropping explosives hither and yon and creating the chaos that is so typical of your culture. That is as good a Christmas tree as ever was, improved even, to take the discordancy away from the poor designs you seem determined to worship."

The telephone rang, interrupting the dispute. Remo answered it. It was Western Union. His Aunt Mildred was going to visit at 9 A.M. She was on her way already.

"Damn," said Remo.

But Chiun ignored him. How could one help someone who failed to appreciate an improved design? How could one reason with such a person? How could one teach such a person? If he wanted one of those ill-formed glaring obscenities sold in stores, then he would have to purchase one himself. It was like giving diamonds to a duck. The duck would prefer grains of corn. Well, let the duck buy its own corn. The Master of Sinanju was not in the duck-feeding business.

"Just got the code from Smitty. We're interrupted again. Our rest period's probably over. Chiun, do you hear me?"

"I do not answer quackings," said the Master of Sinanju and sat, lotus position, in a silence that Remo knew he could never break.

"I'm sorry," said Remo. "Thank you for the tree. It was very kind of you. Thank you again, Little Father."

But there was no answer, and Remo went into the bedroom and lay down for a nap, his last word before dozing being "crap."

He heard the outside door open and was awake as if an alarm had rung. There was some conversing outside in the living room and then a lemon-faced man

22

in gray suit and white shirt with striped green Dartmouth tie entered, carrying a worn leather briefcase. He sat down in a chair.

"What have you done to Chiun? How have you insulted him?" asked Dr. Harold W. Smith.

"I didn't insult him, and what goes on between us is none of your business, Smitty. So what's the urgency?"

"I'd like to advise you again, Remo, how valuable a resource Chiun is and how truly necessary it is for you two to work well together."

"Smitty, you don't understand and I don't think you ever will. Now what's up?"

"It is not nearly as important as your relationship with Chiun. Now, as I gather it, he gave you an important and significant gift which you not only did not receive graciously, but then you refused him some small item which he wanted very much."

"Did you see the bush with the junk on it in the living room?"

"Yes. What happened? It looks like a tornado threw a shrub and some junk through the window. Don't you have maid service? You have the money."

"That's the important and significant gift. Now, have you heard of Barbra Streisand?"

"Yes."

"That's the small item he wants in return," said Remo.

"For certain things," Smith said drily, "we have no dearth of money. And considering how limited we are in personnel on our enforcement arm, we might be able to spare some small amount for Chiun's personal pleasures. Actresses sometimes can be convinced to provide a private service. Not Miss Streisand, of course, but someone comparable."

"He doesn't want to rent her, Smitty."

"He wants to marry?"

"No."

"Then what does he want?"

"He wants to own her."

"Impossible," Smith said.

"Right. Now stick to the things you understand, like everything else."

"Just a minute. You're not going to kidnap her. I mean . . ."

"No. I'm not going to kidnap her. Now what's the latest foul-up I have to compensate for?"

"You know, you're getting as inscrutable as Chiun, and you were never as pleasant."

"Thank you," said Remo, and he sat up to listen. It had been more than a decade since he had gotten his first assignment from this sparse, vinegary man, and in that time, unlike Chiun, he could no longer imagine working for anyone else. He had tried it once* and it was a disaster.

As a Master of Sinanju, Chiun had been trained through centuries of heritage to work for any emperor who would pay the bills of the village of Sinanju. But Remo was not the Master of Sinanju. He had been a simple Newark policeman who was executed publicly and then woke up privately to find himself in a new life. He was to be the killer arm for an organization that did not exist, to help protect a social contract that did not work.**

It was not supposed to be a long tour of duty. The organization had been set up for a just a brief, trying time in the nation's history, that period when the country could not survive within the Constitution. The organization was called CURE. But the fight against

*Destroyer #14, *Judgment Day.*
**Destroyer #1, *Created the Destroyer.*

crime had proved almost unwinnable, and now, ten years later, the secret organization still functioned, its activities known to only two persons: Smith, its director, and Remo, its killer arm. Only those two and whoever happened to be President at the time.

Remo had once asked Smith what would happen if the President decided to stay in office forever, using the organization CURE to cement his power.

"We wouldn't let him," Smith had said.

"What would happen if he decided to expose us? The very admission that we exist would imply the Constitution doesn't work. It'd be chaos."

"The President would appear insane, but because since we don't exist in the first place, we'd be very easy to disband. You're already a dead man, I would remove myself from existence, and no one else knows what we do." Smith said this, but he often wondered himself, and asked Remo if Chiun knew what CURE did.

"Are you still sending the gold to Sinanju on time?" asked Remo.

"Yes."

"Then Chiun couldn't care less what we do."

"That sounds like an answer he would give me," Smith complained.

"What I am saying is that if I told him this was a secret agency to protect the Constitution, he would understand that. If I told him that thousands worked for us without knowing who they worked for, he would understand that. If I told him about the computers at our Folcroft headquarters and how you use them to bribe, extort, pressure and destroy enemies of our Constitution, he could understand that. But there's one thing he could never understand."

"What's that?" Smith had asked timorously.

"The Constitution."

Smith had smiled and then, because he was a thorough man, he had personally explained to the Master of Sinanju about the Constitution of the United States.

Ever since then, Chiun was sure how the United States worked. There was a piece of paper which was a social contract, to which everyone voiced approval and allegiance and to which no one paid any attention.

"It's like your Bible. Pretty songs," Chiun had said; Remo realized that Chiun, in not knowing as others knew, actually did know far, far better.

Now Remo sat on the edge of the bed and listened to the latest assignment which was, as Smith said, only urgent in timing. Whatever the hell that meant.

"We're losing some people within a general point of focus." Smith said.

Remo snapped his fingers. "Of course. Now I've got it."

Smith gave him that "I shall suffer fools gladly" look.

"Now this is where it gets somewhat complicated. In one area of focus, an IRS contingent, we've lost seven men over the last year and a half."

"Why don't you wait until it's five thousand, Smitty, and then you'll have a sure pattern? I mean, why start getting nervous at seven? Where the hell were we at three?"

"Ah, this is where it gets subtle. We're not sure it's seven. We're not sure actually what is happening. Four deaths were, to all appearances, acts of God."

"We can take on God. No trouble," said Remo. "Just find Him for me. Chiun thinks that God doesn't balance well and may leave Himself open even if He is Korean."

"Will you please? We do know that five of the seven, if there were seven, had had attempts made on their lives and that these attempts were unsuccessful, thanks to police efforts. But one died anyway of kidney failure, two of cerebral hemorrhage, one cardiac arrest . . ."

"C'mon, c'mon, get to the point."

"Well, we've just lost this man Boulder who was doing important IRS work. Heart failure during surgery. According to the doctors the appendectomy was a success; the patient died. There's another man in his line of work that we'd like to keep alive and we think we might have trouble doing that."

"Sure," Remo said. "I'll do it. Easy. I'll make sure he keeps a low cholesterol count and exercises regularly. Then I'll reinforce his heart and lungs."

"That's not the point. I just want to make sure that a building doesn't fall on him or a car doesn't hit him."

"And what happens if he has a heart attack?"

"We're not sure about those acts of God I mentioned. We want you to find out. We want you to keep this man alive. We want you to protect him from forces known and unknown. You will make sure over a period—let's say a month—that nothing happens to him. If someone does attempt something, stop it, perhaps run it to its source, pack your bags and go back to your rest. Clear?"

"As it's going to be. Clear as it's going to be. If it gets any clearer to me, I'll need a seeing-eye dog to find it."

"You know, Remo, as you grow older I understand you less and less."

"I was about to say that of you, Smitty."

"I haven't changed since I was fifteen, Remo."

"I believe that," said Remo, and then got the fix on the man he was supposed to protect. His name was Nathan David Wilberforce and he lived in Scranton. With his mother. He didn't like loud noises.

CHAPTER THREE

There were three excellent reasons why the treasury agents should leave the Wilberforce household immediately. Mrs. Wilberforce said she would make them perfectly clear, if the agents would sit down—no, not on the couch, couldn't they see it had a dust cover on it, no, not on the hideabed, that was for company—well, then, if they must, stand.

"You have come into my house, bringing filth from the streets, putting your hats wherever they fall and using vile and obscene terms in front of Nathan David. You stressed there were dangers to Nathan David and you were protecting him. But who will protect Nathan David from dirt, untidiness and obscenity? Certainly not you three," said Mrs. Wilberforce in righteous indignation, her massive breastworks rising under the flopping brown bouclé dress like unscalable fortifications. She stood six-foot-one and weighed, according to the agents' best guesses, a healthy two hundred and forty pounds. That she had not played defensive tackle for the Pittsburgh Steelers, said one of the agents outside her hearing, was that she probably didn't like the untidiness of the locker rooms.

"Ma'am, your son is an assistant director of the

IRS. He is a very important person and we have reason to believe his life may be in danger."

"I know he's in danger. From riff-raff."

"We discovered someone working on the front of Assistant Director Wilberforce's car last month. He was not installing a new muffler, ma'am, if I may be blunt. He was working on the brakes."

"You don't know what he was installing. You didn't catch him."

"We stopped him, ma'am."

"Good for you. Nathan David will take buses from here on in. If that will make you happy?"

"Not exactly, ma'am. We just want to be sure. We have our orders to function as sort of a screen for Assistant Director Wilberforce. He is working on very, very sensitive projects, and we would appreciate your cooperation. It's for his own good."

"I will decide what is good for Nathan David."

"We have our orders, ma'am."

But when the agents checked with the office that afternoon, they found that their orders were changed, and they assumed that Mrs. Wilberforce, of 832 Vandalia Avenue, had some form of influence. They were yanked from the case immediately.

"Don't ask me," said their supervisor. "The change came from higher up. I can't explain it."

When the three agents said goodbye to Assistant Director Wilberforce in his office, Wilberforce was interviewing a new employee, a thinnish sort of man with high cheekbones and very thick wrists.

"We just came in to say goodbye and wish you luck, Mr. Wilberforce."

"Oh, thank you. Thank you very much," said Wilberforce. "Thank you. I'd shake hands, but you're at the door already."

"You never shook hands, Mr. Wilberforce," said the agent who acted as spokesman.

"Well, why start now?" said Wilberforce and smiled nervously. He was a neat, plumpish man in his middle forties and his desk was painfully neat, as though the papers had been placed there with surveying instruments.

When the agents had left, Remo put his feet on the desk.

"Sir. Uh, sir. That's my desk," said Wilberforce.

"Good. I'll just sit here and not bother you."

"I believe that if you are going to work for me, we should at least come to some sort of understanding. I like things neat."

Remo looked at his shoes. They were shined. He looked up to Wilberforce, puzzled.

"My desk. Your feet are on my desk."

"Right," said Remo.

"Would you mind taking them off?"

"Uh, yeah," said Remo softly.

"Would you please take them off?"

"No," said Remo.

"Well, then, I insist you take them off. I can get very physical, Mr. Remo. And it would do very little good for your government career if I should be forced to take extreme measures."

Remo shrugged and his feet rose a quarter of an inch above the desk while he continued to sit in front of it. Wilberforce was confident this new employee would have to lower his feet to the floor. Even a dancer couldn't keep them raised like that for more than a minute or two. But as the interview went into its second hour, the feet did not lower and the new employee seemed unstrained. The feet remained there, that quarter-inch above the desk, as if they were nailed in space.

The new employee had a special function. He was a time-study man. It was his job to find out why Mr. Wilberforce's unit worked so well and then make this information available to others. He would have to stay fairly close to Mr. Wilberforce to see how he allocated his time and rest, even to the hours he slept.

Wilberforce asked about Mr. Remo's background in time study, but got vague answers. He asked about Mr. Remo's training but got vague answers. He wanted to phone his director and register a complaint about insolence on the job, but he never seemed to be free of this man long enough to make a private phone call.

As usual, Wilberforce worked late, so that when he left, the outside office was dark. The hallway on the eighth floor of the federal building was dark. Black. The hallway smelled of fresh disinfectant from a recent evening mopping.

"The elevator is down there to the left," said Wilberforce.

"There are usually lights in the hallway, aren't there?" asked the time-study man.

"Yes. Don't be nervous. Just hold on to my han . . . uh, stay close to the wall and follow my voice."

"Why don't you follow me?" said Remo.

"But you can't see the elevator."

"Don't worry. I see more than you."

It was then that Wilberforce realized he could not hear the new employee's breathing. He knew this was strange because he could hear his own so well. He did not even hear the employee's steps on the marble floor, yet his own sounded like rifle shots in the silent hallway. It was as if the employee had disappeared in the darkness.

Wilberforce moved toward the elevator and when

31

he went to the other side of the hall to feel for the elevator button, he heard feet moving rapidly. Perhaps two or three men close by, and then he heard what sounded like the puncturing of paper bags, a throat gurgle and one fast flight of birds. Right by his head.

Then the hall lights came on. Wilberforce gasped and felt his head become light. His new employee was standing beside him holding his arm so he would not faint. Wilberforce had seen it.

The elevator door had been open. And there was no elevator. He was standing before an open shaft. There were eight floors of nothing before him.

"My god. Someone could have fallen in. What carelessness. What carelessness," gasped Wilberforce.

"Someone did," said his new employee and held him while he leaned over the edge for a look.

Down below in the darkness, Wilberforce made out a broken body impaled on the springs and perhaps two others. He could see only arms and legs way down there, and then he saw something floating down toward the bodies. It was his late afternoon snack.

Remo helped Wilberforce to the stairs, and they walked down the eight flights. At each landing, Wilberforce gathered a bit more of his horrified senses. By the ground floor, he was complaining about the lack of proper maintenance in federal buildings. His mind had done what Remo had heard Chiun say untrained minds did. When confronted by an unacceptable fact, it would rearrange it to make it acceptable or it would ignore it.

Standing in the Scranton street with Pennsylvania snow falling, turning from white to gray in the last twenty feet of its descent, Remo saw that Wilberforce had adjusted the attempted assassination into a janitorial problem.

"I'll have to send a memo to the building superintendent in the morning," said Wilberforce, buttoning his gray and orange winter overcoat, the kind of coat Remo knew was destined second-hand for Skid Row, but which he had never seen worn new before.

Remo wore gray slacks, a light blue shirt, and a gray-blue blazer that flapped in the wind.

"Where's your coat?" asked Wilberforce.

"I don't have one," said Remo.

"You can afford one, can't you?"

"Yeah. I don't need one."

"That's impossible. It's cold out."

"How do you know it's cold?"

"The temperature tells me," said Wilberforce.

"Well, talk back to it. Tell it it's wrong."

"You can't do that to temperature. It's part of nature."

"What do you think you are? You're part of nature."

"I am Nathan David Wilberforce and I keep buttoned up," said Wilberforce. "I see that your mother hasn't properly trained you."

"I never knew my mother. I was raised in an orphanage," said Remo.

"I'm sorry," said Wilberforce. "I can't imagine what life would be like without a mother."

"Pretty good," said Remo.

"That's a horrible thing to say," said Wilberforce. "I don't know what I'd do without my mother."

"You might do pretty well, Wilberforce."

"You're a horrid human being," said Wilberforce.

"If you work at it, you might become one, too," said Remo. "A human being, that is."

"Is your work over for the day or are you going to report on my homelife tonight?"

"Tonight isn't so important, but I might as well take a look-see."

"You don't take notes."

"In my head," said Remo. "I take notes in my head."

That night would not be dangerous for Wilberforce, Remo knew. It would be probably one of the safer nights for him. In the Western world, as Chiun had taught him, there were only single attacks, never multiple level on a linear time basis. Chiun had explained it in the earliest training using lacquered wooden balls the size of grapes and a large wooden ball about the size and color of a grapefruit.

"In the West, an assassination is one ball," said Chiun, holding up a single, small black ball in his bony hands. The ball seemed to rise to the tips of his fingernails as if on a string.

"The philosophy behind this must come from the mind of a businessman for it is not really designed for effectiveness. It is designed to use as little energy as possible. Watch."

Chiun pointed to the large yellow ball on the table. "That is the target. When it is on the floor, the task is done. For that is what assassination is: a task."

"Call it what it really is," Remo had said. "Killing. Murder. Say it if you're going to say it. Don't give me this funny talk about a task."

Chiun had nodded patiently. It was only years later, after Remo achieved proficiency and wisdom that had made him into another being, that Chiun would criticize and call him a pale piece of a pig's ear. In the early training, Chiun appeared to be patient.

"Pay attention," Chiun said. "This is the Western technique."

34

Chiun flipped the small black ball at the larger yellow ball. It struck slightly off-center and the larger ball moved slightly toward the edge of the table. Chiun's hands came to rest on the lap of his golden kimono and exaggeratedly he watched the large ball. Then, with just as much exaggeration, he appeared to ponder, and then flipped another black ball. It missed. He stared at the large yellow ball, appeared to think long and hard, then threw another small black ball. This one hit the larger ball dead center, and slapped it over the edge of the table onto the floor. The smaller ball, spinning wildly with English, rolled almost crazily around the table, but then wound up stopping just before Chiun's hand.

"Western technique," Chiun said. "Now the technique of Sinanju. Get me the yellow ball."

Remo picked up the large ball, bending with pain to reach it—for he was in the early phase of his physical training—and put it back on the table.

Chiun bowed, smiled, reached into his pocket and brought forth a handful of small black balls. He took a few in each hand, and then snaked his two hands in different directions in front of the table, and then, bing, bing, bing, bing, balls shot out from his fingertips as it from two rocket launchers, and one after another, hit the large yellow ball dead center, without pause, and spun it immediately off the edge of the table.

Chiun put his now empty hands on his lap again.

"Now do you understand? The Western way of assassination provides moments of readjustment, secure periods, awareness of danger time—all things that you do not wish for the intended target."

"How did you do that with the balls? Shoot them out of your hands that way? Like little bullets, and your fingers didn't even seem to move."

35

"Do you wish to be a juggler or an assassin?"

"And that ball that came back to you? Did you have reverse English on that or what?" Remo had asked.

"It is not the ball that I wish you to understand but the method. Some day you may learn."

"Do you think if I grew my fingernails longer I could do that with those balls?" asked Remo.

Chiun sighed.

Remo babbled on. "If I'm going to make a hit on someone, and I'm not sure that I'm ever going to, I'm going to use the biggest gun I can get. Now show me how you do that thing with the balls. Is it with your wrist?" Remo had said. It was later, as he began to understand Chiun's training and as his body came to be a different kind of instrument, that he found one day he could do with the balls just what Chiun had done. It came not from trickery, but from knowledge and feel of the essence of the balls. And Remo never forgot Chiun's lesson on the Western and Eastern assassination techniques.

Now as Remo and Wilberforce approached Wilberforce's 1957 Volkswagen, Remo had little concern for the evening. Wilberforce might even have two days, but at this moment, he was as safe as he was ever going to be. Western assassination attempts came one at a time.

Wilberforce opened the hood over the rear engine.

"If you remember those three men who came in earlier today, they were bodyguards and they always checked the rear of my car. I really don't know what to look for. Perhaps you do."

"Yes, I do," said Remo, getting into the front of the car.

Wilberforce left the engine open and unlocked the driver's door and poked his head into the front seat.

"Well, take a look then. Come on out and look."

"I know without looking. Whatever those body-guards used to look for is not there."

"How do you know that?"

"Remember the men at the bottom of the elevator shaft?"

"Don't remind me of that."

"Well, their eyes weren't slanted."

"What does that mean?"

"It means that your engine is as safe now as it is ever going to be. C'mon, shut the trunk, and let's take a look at your house."

On the way to the Wilberforce home, a seven-room white Colonial with green shutters and an infinitesimal lawn now occupied by a strip of gray Scranton snow, Wilberforce wanted to know from his new employee what he had meant by the men's eyes and how he got into the car when the door was locked.

"The lock doesn't work," said Remo. And this was slightly honest because the lock no longer did work, now that Remo had broken it.

"Now about the eyes?"

"It has to do with multiple attacks as opposed to singular, which allow defensive reaction time. The men were Western and therefore singular."

"I see. That explains it," said Wilberforce. He had spent eighteen years working for the government and had become expert at appearing to understand things.

Mrs. Wilberforce took one look at her son's companion, standing there in the snow without an over-coat, and asked Nathan David where he had met this person.

"Sort of an employee, Mummy. He's making a study of my department in an effort to determine why we do things so well."

"He does things well," said Mrs. Wilberforce, looking down at Remo, "because he was brought up well. If everyone were brought up well, this country would work well."

"May I come in?" asked Remo, skirting the massive person in front of him.

"You there," barked Mrs. Wilberforce. "You did not have permission to enter. Go back to the doorway."

Remo checked the living room, an overly neat expanse of overstuffed furniture, unworn old rugs, ugly ceramic lamps and doodads.

"I said, out of my house until you have permission. You there, you're not listening to me."

The dining room was another grotesque collection of early American furniture, well preserved.

"Either you're out of this house in one minute or I call the authorities. The authorities, young man. The authorities."

The kitchen had a gas-stove, one 1940s refrigerator, and more doodads. Something meaty was cooking for supper. Remo heard the galumphing stride of Mrs. Wilberforce behind him. He stepped left, the mass of humanity went with the step and he calmly walked out of the kitchen to the stairs. Mrs. Wilberforce's room was another clutter; the bed was single. Her son's room looked like a Wall Street law office with an oak post bed in it. There was a guest room as inviting as a dungeon and two bathrooms.

Remo skirted Mrs. Wilberforce climbing up the steps by hopping over the railing mid-stairway. Nearby was the basement door. In the basement he found exactly where the next attack would take place. The oil burner.

According to Smith, there had been an attempt on Wilberforce's brakes earlier. Tonight it had been an elevator out of service. The pattern of simulated accidents would probably continue at least one more time. And a wooden house with an oil burner was just fine. Night would be ideal. Fire begins in the basement, cutting off the bottom floor escape. Wilberforces asleep upstairs. Nice, thought Remo. For peo- who worked with gadgets.

There would not be another attempt this evening; the men were Western. He had known they were Western even before he had heard them in the hallway. He could smell them. One, he had seen later when looking down the shaft, had been black, but contrary to some Western opinion, the odors of black and white were identical. People smelled of what they ate and the attackers had been three heavy meat eaters. Their pores reeked of it. Beef, beef and beef. Sometimes Remo wanted a hamburger, remembering its delicious meaty taste and thinking of the onions and the tomato ketchup, and how good it would be to eat one again. But now when he got close to the smell, he was repulsed. He had smelled that odor in the dark hallway and taken the three men, using one as the bumper to guide the other two into the shaft whose very openness Remo had heard. He finished the one he used as a bumper with a simple brain stroke. If he had just thrown him still alive into the shaft, one of the other two might have cushioned his fall.

Granted he should have saved one. But there would be another attempt on Wilberforce, and in the hallway of the federal building, Wilberforce would have been a nuisance, and might just have wound up falling into the open shaft himself. Remo would wait for the next attempt, follow it to its source, find out what was what, report to Smith and return to his rest period without Wilberforce being any the wiser, other than being relieved of a time-study man he didn't want in the first place.

"You down there. If you're not out in five seconds, I will phone the police. Do you hear me?" It was Mrs. Wilberforce.

Okay, it was the boiler. Tomorrow night or the next. Not tonight. Remo glided up the basement steps, underneath Mrs. Wilberforce's outstretched arm. He gave the massive corseted rump a little pat as he passed her and heard a yell of horror, as if he had disemboweled someone.

"Aaarrrrghhh," yelled Mrs. Wilberforce. Nathan David hid behind the couch. Had Remo's pat done that? He skirted the large flailing arms to get a better view of Mrs. Wilberforce's rump. It seemed in fine condition. Not even a thread was disjointed. And he knew for sure it had been just a pat.

Remo moved around a knee kick, and to make sure of what he had heard he gave the fanny another pat.

"Aaarrgghhhh. Animal. Pig. Animal. Rape!" yelled Mrs. Wilberforce.

"Merry Christmas," said Remo and, moving inside a left hook, gave Mrs. Wilberforce a wet kiss on the cheek.

"Good night, Nathan David," said Remo. He left the Wilberforce house filled with good cheer.

CHAPTER FOUR

"I don't like fire," said Anthony Stace, also known as Anselmo Stacio and, to many people who had never met him and knew neither of his names, as "Mr. Big."

In Scranton, Mr. Stace was president of Stace Realty, a director of the First National Agricultural Bank and Trust Company, chairman of the United Charities, and the man to see if you were starting a fund drive for your church or club. Mr. Stace was rarely known to say "no."

In another level of Scranton, Anselmo Stacio kept tight and orderly control of the numbers, sports gambling, trucking, several labor unions and a goodly share of those sorts of loans where the repayment was seven dollars for five per week and the collateral was your body—its health and well-being.

It was said by those very few who knew both his roles that Stacio did more good for the community than Stace. Stacio kept the white powder out of Scranton and its environs. Heroin, he had said, tended to create disorder and in disorder people often wanted drastic change. Since things were very profitable the way they were, both Anthony Stace and Anselmo

Stacio wanted very little change. Especially since they had created a brilliant financial relationship.

As director of the First Aggie, Stace had access to large amounts of capital. As Don Anselmo, Stacio had access to high-yield investments. For at seven-for-five per week, Stacio could put Stace's money to work in loans that far outstripped the yields of Xerox and Polaroid. The First Aggie was a loan-shark funnel and at times banked half the state's under-the-counter loans. First Aggie had more money "on the street" in the area than the Federal Reserve Board.

It was a fine working relationship for the one man with two names, until a piddling assistant director of the Internal Revenue Service began collecting data. And what was worse, this piddling assistant director, Nathan David Wilberforce, was an unreasonable man.

When Wilberforce's account showed he had a savings balance of $125,000, up $123,547 from the week before, he brought it to the First Aggie's attention, both in a registered letter and personally. The senior vice president was shocked that such a mistake could occur. The president was shocked that such a mistake could occur. It was such a shocking mistake that a member of the board of directors, Anthony Stace himself, personally visited the Wilberforce home to express his concern.

He paid homage to the fine Wilberforce home and its beautiful decorations and Mrs. Wilberforce bemoaned the fact that so few gentlemen like Mr. Stace were around anymore. Mr. Stace asked Nathan David Wilberforce when he first realized there had been a mistake.

"When I made a $23 deposit by mail and the book came back $125,000. Well, I told your teller, Mrs. V. Hansen, that there must be some mistake. She

42

wasn't rude but there was a touch of surliness to her voice, an unmistakable tone of surliness."

"We'll have to look into that," said Stace, carefully resting his gray homburg on his lap. He was a dignified man with graying hair and lines of integrity in his face. His brown eyes showed warmth and trust. His dark gray suit was cut more for neatness than for style.

He said he would see that Mrs. V. Hansen was made aware of his concern over possible rudeness to a treasured client. And then a wonderful idea came to Mr. Anthony Stace. He knew where the money might have come from. It might not have been a mistake at all.

"Sometimes, Mr. Wilberforce, people are so grateful for favors that they make secret gifts to a person's bank account. Have you done any favors for people lately?"

Wilberforce thought hard. "I did promote a secretary two grades instead of one, but she was a tremendous worker. It was part of a new promotion enrichment program. But I don't think she would give me $123,547 in gratitude. The increase amounted to $900 a year and at that rate it would take more than a century to make up, and if you consider the interest, it would never be made up. As a matter of fact, it would fall behind at a compounding rate of about $4,000 a year."

"You work for the government then, Mr. Wilberforce," said Anthony Stace, who knew damn well where Mr. Wilberforce worked.

"Internal Revenue."

"Assistant director," said Mrs. Wilberforce.

"Perhaps in your job you have done someone a favor that he wishes to repay."

"Impossible," said Wilberforce.

"Perhaps it is a payment for future favors."

"Impossible again. That would be bribery."

"Of course," said Stace. "I do believe that's against the law."

"I probably shouldn't even tell you this, but there are people at your bank who are under investigation right now," Wilberforce said. "Maybe it came from one of them."

"Investigation? What sort of investigation?" asked Stace, his brows furrowing in deep concern.

"Oh, I can't reveal that. I just thought you should be put on notice how this extra-large deposit may have occurred."

"I'm glad you told me. Our reputation is our main asset."

"Now, don't worry. It's nothing that would incriminate your whole bank. Just sort of a few rotten apples in the barrel. But I can't tell you anything more."

"Of course, I wouldn't expect you to," said Stace, who complimented Mrs. Wilberforce on her son's integrity. It was, he said, the sort of integrity they were always looking for at the First National Agricultural Bank and Trust Company, particularly in vice presidents, and there would soon be an opening, but of course Mr. Wilberforce could not consider such a thing. Of course, Wilberforce said that he could not.

Four hours later, Bonifacio Palumbo and Salvatore Messina were adjusting the brakes on a 1957 Volkswagen so they would not brake. They were interrupted by three armed men, waving guns and badges. Palumbo and Messina fled, reporting to the man who hired them that they had not been able to finish the job. He, in turn, reported to someone else, who reported to someone else, and that someone else finally told Stace.

After a week's deliberation, another order funneled

through the protective layers of Stace's empire. The operation took seven days to plan, three days to prepare, and 3.9 seconds to fail, counting elevator shaft time for Moe Klein, Johnny (The Pig) Pigellino and Willie (Sweet Willie) Williams. Stace naturally did not attend their funerals. He didn't even know the men.

So on a very cold day, Anthony Stace donned the hat of Anselmo Stacio and brought a problem to a close friend in New York City.

"I don't like fires," said Stacio. "I never liked fires. They're uncontrollable. They're destructive of property." He was in the living room of an old friend, who was also a man of repute, with great influence. He was an older man and he wore a thin gray sweater and a white shirt buttoned up to his neck. His wife brought him little cups of tea and for Stacio, a glass of anisette, which he sipped as he sought this man's advice.

The house appeared much like any other brownstone on Eastern Parkway in Brooklyn. The only difference was that instead of Feldman or Moskowitz, the owner's name was Scubisci. Pietro Scubisci, a good neighbor and a reasonable man.

"You don't like fires, I don't like fires," said Scubisci. "You don't like blood; I don't like blood. I do not even like harsh words and I am sure neither do you. But life is not an easy thing and a man does not always have a choice as to the comfort with which he will make his living. Given a choice, I would not even be Pietro Scubisci. I would be Nelson Rockefeller, and if I were Rockefeller I would not be in politics but would sit on a sunny island and watch the birds fly by."

"I would restructure the Chase Manhattan Bank," said Stacio, smiling.

"But we are not Rockefellers. So there are things we must do that we do not like. Even the Rockefellers must do things they do not like."

"I have heard that there might be another way," said Stacio.

"There are always other ways," said Scubisci.

"As you know, Don Pietro, and this is no reflection upon you, I have a quiet domain and the need for blood is less than in your area."

"You run a good business, Anselmo."

"Thank you," said Stacio. "Therefore I am not fully aware of what may be the latest methods."

"Since the gun, what new methods are there? Really? Nothing new in a hundred years."

"I have heard of a new way, Don Pietro. A way in which all appears very natural, like an unfortunate happenstance."

Don Pietro leaned forward. He whispered. "Are you talking about the hospital?"

"Is that what it is?"

Don Pietro slowly lowered his head and nodded. "Too much money. Too expensive. Fire. Take fire. What would it cost if a whole block burned down? You're a businessman. What would it cost? Besides, the hospital people, they squeeze your *gagliones*. Hard."

"With all due respect, Don Pietro, I would like to investigate the possibilities of this hospital. It may be a very neat way of solving my problem."

Stacio listened to whom he must see, how he must approach that person and took one more bit of cautious advice before he left the Scubisci home. From Kennedy Airport, he made a long-distance call to the Robler Clinic, outside Baltimore.

"This is Anthony Stace. I'm president of Stace Realty and a director of the First National Agricultural Bank and Trust Company of Scranton. I'd like to talk to your assistant administrator, Ms. Kathleen Hahl."

"She's busy right now. Can she return your call, sir?"

"I'm on a flight now to Baltimore," said Stace. "I hope she can see me. I'd like to discuss a sizeable contribution. Sizeable."

"I'll give Ms. Hahl the message, sir. Is Ms. Hahl expecting you?"

"No."

"You'll have to make an appointment."

"But this is a sizeable contribution."

"We appreciate that, sir, but Ms. Hahl is a busy person."

"When can I make an appointment?"

"This is mid-December. Perhaps the end of January."

"You mean I have to get on line to make a contribution? I'm the head of the United Charities and I've never heard of anything like that."

"I'm sorry, sir. I'm just Ms. Hahl's secretary."

"Well, if I were to fly in today, would it be possible for her to see me just for a few minutes?" said Stace angrily.

"Possibly. I can't guarantee that, sir. How do you spell your name?"

"Stace. S as in sizzling, T as in truculent, A as in angry, C as in crotchety, and E as in enraged."

"Just a minute, sir, will you hold on?"

Stace held on through $1.75 worth of quarters, dimes and nickels before charging the call to his office phone in Scranton. Finally, the secretary returned to the phone.

"Ms. Hahl says she will be glad to see you this afternoon, Mr. Stacio," said the secretary. Stace found himself listening to a dead line and wondering how the girl knew his other name.

In Baltimore, he took a cab from the airport to the Robler Clinic. He had encountered many a put-down artist in his career and the most effective of them had a purpose. Obviously Ms. Hahl wanted to put him at an emotional disadvantage by disclosing quickly that she and her people were aware of his other name. Well, that showed they were what Don Pietro said they were, the kind who would squeeze your balls—and hard! But then, perhaps, they were a bit unwise. Perhaps they gave away too much over the telephone. He would find out quickly enough. After all, Ms. Hahl was only a woman, and while women were nice and sometimes even very bright, it was not for no reason that the slang word for strength and courage was balls.

Stace was not prepared, however, for what he found in the Robler Clinic's Office of Development. He was not prepared for Ms. Kathleen Hahl. His mouth opened in surprise when he saw her sitting behind a large glass-topped desk with the capital campaign arrow behind her head. She didn't belong there. She belonged in Hollywood. She was beautiful.

Rich chestnut hair gave the exquisite fine soft features a halo of loveliness. The lips were full and moist; the smile a jewel of grace. Her eyes were brown and soft, soft as her body which was tantalizingly full, just short of plump. A thin white blouse with the top two buttons unfastened gave a hint of rising breasts.

Stace reminded himself he was there for business.

"I'm here to talk about a contribution," he said. He sat down in front of the desk.

"Your hat. Can I do something with your hat?" She reached across the desk and Stace smelled a teasing perfume, not quite rich but definitely strong, like a hint of the old Jamaica rum combined with the freshness of the sea.

His hands became moist. He did not rise to hand her his hat because rising might disclose what would be an embarrassment at this point. At other times, he was quite proud of his instant ability to achieve this state of arousal, but now he wanted to talk business.

"No, no. I'll hold my hat. Thanks. I'd like to talk about money."

"Why, Mr. Stacio. Or Stace, whichever you wish. You know in fund raising, we never mention money. We have leadership support, advancement support, we have chairmanships and vice chairmanships, we have goals and even special funds, but the word we never use is money."

"How much?" asked Stace.

"How much for what, Mr. Stacio?"

"For Nathan David Wilberforce, assistant director of Internal Revenue, Scranton. How much?"

"You're creating support leadership in his name?"

"Is that what you call it?"

"That's what we call money. What you want we call murder."

"Whatever, lady, how much?"

"You give us no warning, you pop in without references so we had to check you ourselves and then you right out ask us to kill someone. Now is that any way to do business, Mr. Stacio?" She unbuttoned the next button and eased a hand under her blouse. Her tongue touched her upper lip.

Stace, for all his fifty-five years, felt charged as he had not since he was a teenager. The heat hung in his throat. He cleared his throat but the heat was still there.

"Don't play games. How much?"

"One million dollars."

"What kind of shit is that? I wouldn't pay one million to kill the pope."

"This is a volunteer program, Mr. Stacio. We're not asking you for one million. You came to us. You came here. Feel free to leave and never return."

Stace watched the hand move inside the bra, and then lower the strap off her shoulder. Through the blouse, he could see the rising red cone of her breast, like an aroused tower.

"Am I distracting you, Mr. Stacio?"

"You know damn well you are."

"Then hop in. C'mon."

"How much?"

"No charge, Mr. Stacio. I'm just looking for a man to satisfy me. I've never found one. C'mon. You won't last more than twenty seconds anyhow."

"Bitch," snarled Stace. Without taking off coat or vest or even pants, he unzipped, ready and full, and charged around the desk.

Kathy Hahl raised her legs, laughing. He saw she wore no panties and then they were joined, her legs around his back, his knees against the seat of the chair. She was moist and ready and she felt warm, incredibly warm around him.

"One one thousand, two one thousand, three one thousand, four one thousand, five one thousand," she said. She was laughing and looking at her watch.

Stace steeled his will. He steeled it to think of billiard balls and baseball bats, but that didn't help at all. Then he thought of ceiling lights, funerals, of construction plans and plumbing fixtures, of the most frightening moment of his life. He was fifty-five years old. He wasn't a kid anymore. He shouldn't be worrying about this sort of thing anymore. He was a respected businessman.

And then he felt her muscles close around him briefly and release and there was that tickle. And p'doom, he was spent.

"Eighteen one thousand," said Kathy Hahl. She locked her legs closed around his waist. "Now let's talk. We can offer you a leadership program where your support level can be geared to your need. But the plan is one million dollars. If you want to participate."

"That's a hell of a lot of money," said Stace, who now felt the pain in his back from leaning over. His head was flushed and his heart was beating rapidly. He thought Kathy Hahl had a beautiful nose. He saw it very close.

"Is it really? We know you are in that income bracket. It's not an unreasonable package." She patted the side of his head tenderly, straightening a strand of hair.

"That's a hell of a lot for a hit," he said.

"Yes."

"I want to try something else first."

"You've tried something else. If it had worked, you wouldn't be here." She looked at him coolly.

"Suppose I said yes. How do you know I'd give you the money?"

"We would see that you did."

"Suppose I just take care of you? You do the job, I owe you a million, and I settle with someone for a reasonable five or six grand, which is the going rate. Let's say you're super-super difficult. Twenty-five grand tops, outside. Twenty-five grand. You're gone, and there's no one I owe a million to."

"It sounds like you may have done something like that before," said Kathy Hahl, reaching behind Stace and, with her left hand, twirling a ring she wore on her right.

"Maybe," he said. He shook his head. "A million's too much. I'd like to try something else first."

She shrugged.

"My back hurts, let go," said Stace.

Kathy Hahl smiled at him and snaked her hands inside the back of his trousers, reached down to his bare buttocks and pulled him in closer to her body. He felt a small stinging in his left rump. She squeezed him once more with her legs, and then he felt the legs unlock and he straightened up and rubbed his back. He put everything in order, then zipped and felt relieved that there were no stains. His composure was not only restored; he felt it enhanced. She had given him her body and he had taken it, but he had stuck to his guns and refused to go for the million dollars. To hell with it. Don Pietro might be right. Fire might be better.

With a brush of her skirt, Kathleen Hahl was sitting straight again behind the desk like a businesswoman. She was smiling at him. He felt sorry for her.

"Look," he said, "I'm sorry we can't deal. But I would like to give the hospital something anyway. What would be fair?"

She looked at her watch. "Eighteen thousand dollars. For eighteen seconds."

"Agreed. Make it out to the hospital?"

"No. To me."

"I'd pay that for a good lay," said Stace haughtily.

"So would I," said Ms. Kathleen Hahl. "If I ever found one."

He wrote her a check. She took it, checked the amount, put it in her desk drawer and asked him, "Do you ever have headaches?"

"Never."

"A first time for everything," she said.

Later that night in Scranton, Anselmo Stacio made arrangements for Marvin (The Torch), but he cut short the discussion with his top layer of middlemen. He had a severe headache. Just before he went to bed, the butler inquired if Mr. Stace would like a sedative.

"No thank you," said Stace.

"Perhaps I should call a doctor, sir?"

"No, no, not a doctor," said Stace, remembering the hospital. "Definitely not a doctor."

CHAPTER FIVE

"Tonight's the night, Little Father," said Remo, dissolving the last grains of rice in his mouth to liquid, and then swallowing. He took his plate to the bathroom and flushed into the sewer system of the Holiday Inn the trout almandine and asparagus blanketed by rich golden Hollandaise sauce He had learned long ago that one does not order a bowl of rice and a piece of raw fish or steamed duck at a mass-market restaurant. That had been a complication in itself. How much easier it was to order a meal with rice and then eat some of the rice, disposing of the meal. He never ordered beef because sometimes the juices spilled into the rice and in beef, as in much other food, the flavor was often enhanced with monosodium glutamate.

Some people got numb and sick when they ate monosodium glutamate. With his nervous system, Remo had once gone into shock. The chemical was a strong poison to him, one of the few his body was unable to reject.

Chiun, on the other hand, decried the waste of food, saying that if there had been plentiful food there never would have been a House of Sinanju.

"Well then, aren't you lucky," Remo had answered.

"No," said Chiun. "For all the wonder of the House of Sinanju, nevertheless it comes from pain and fear and hunger. The House of Sinanju was born in the crops that failed."

"You left out greed, Little Father. You know your ancestors did pretty well in Persia, and with all your fourteen steamer trunks we have to take everywhere, you're pretty rich by Korean standards."

"Greed comes from the memory of hunger. It is another form of fear. My richness, my true richness, is as yours—our discipline. You have nothing but that."

"I can get all the cash I want from Upstairs."

"And what have you bought with all this cash from Upstairs?"

"I don't need anything. If I want something, I get it. We move around a lot."

"You will always be rich from a rich country because you never hunger for things."

"I was raised in a frigging orphanage. By nuns. I had nothing. Nothing."

"You ate?"

"Yes."

"And slept in a bed?"

"Yes."

"Then, like others in your country, you do not know the rest of the world. You create crisis from inconvenience and never know real crisis. Yours is a rich and blessed country with sharing that has never been known before. Though priests and shamans and kings declare it as a goal, nowhere—nowhere—has there ever been so much for so many. Nowhere and never."

"Yeah, we're pretty good, Little Father."

"Pretty good? What have you done for it, other than appear from the right womb in the right country during the right century? You have done nothing."

"All this over a frigging lamb chop," Remo said.

"I have seen men kill for smaller pieces of meat," Chiun said and righteously turned on his special television receiver which stored on tape concurrently running daytime serials, an art form that Chiun called "the only expression of beauty in a gross land" and that Remo called "those stupid soaps."

It had not seemed right to the Master of Sinanju that those dramas should be shown simultaneously so that a person would be denied one if he watched another. Upstairs fixed it so that while Chiun watched one, all the others were taped, and he alone in all the land was able to watch an uninterrupted four hours daily starting with "As the Planet Revolves" at noon and ending with "The Young and the Drastic" at 4 P.M.

Occasionally, there would be accidental interruptions by people crossing before the television screen and sometimes even turning off the set.* These interruptions lasted only that millisecond that it took the long-nailed hands of Chiun to strike. Then Remo would have to dispose of the bodies. As Chiun explained it—he could explain everything so that he was free of guilt—all that had happened was that a frail, gentle, wise old man had been restored his brief moments of pleasure.

"In America, we call it murder," Remo said.

"In America, you have many strange names for things," Chiun had said. He also always refused to help clean up the bodies, under the supposition that Remo was the pupil and the little tidying up needed around their domiciles was his responsibility. Besides, had Remo ever once heard him ask one of the victims

*Destroyer #4, *Mafia Fix.*

to interrupt the meager pleasures of his television dramas? It was an unprovoked assault upon a peaceful old man which was met in kind.

One did not interrupt Chiun's shows and one did not throw away food. Therefore, Remo prudently avoided even talking during the soaps and never threw food away in front of Chiun. He shut the bathroom door when he flushed it down the toilet.

"Tonight's the night. I feel it," said Remo again. He was testing to see if Chiun had gotten over the Christmas tree—Barbra Streisand incident or, as Chiun had referred to it once on the way from San Francisco to Pennsylvania, "the heart-rending insult." Remo was not quite sure how Chiun had translated the facts into his own thinking but somehow the feeding of ducks had gotten into it and there were, between the long periods of silence, comments about corn, something being fit for ducks, and the quackings of the American way of life, with Remo being the repository of its most grievous flaws.

Now Chiun said, "Remember, you represent the teaching of Sinanju. Sloppiness and careless technique do not enhance Sinanju."

Remo felt good. There would be comments somewhere down the line establishing that Chiun was the injured party, but to all intents and purposes the incident was over. The criticism about technique was a sign that all was forgiven. Forgotten, never, but forgiven.

"Little Father, I was wondering the other day," Remo said. "I was thinking back to those early days and the balls twirling over the table as a demonstration of the Western and Eastern attacks and while I see now how foolish I was in looking at the spinning of the balls instead of what you were trying to show, another idea came to me."

"Better than the first, I hope."

"Perhaps. What I was thinking was that if we have mastery like that and if your ancestors had mastery like that, then why couldn't your ancestors have supported Sinanju by magic tricks or even the playing of games of chance, which in their hands would not be games of chance at all?"

"I too wondered that once," Chiun said, "and the Master who trained me showed me dice. He told me he would first slap me and then teach me how to make whatever numbers I wished appear on top. For that is how dice are scored, not by the numbers that appear on the sides or on the bottom, but . . ."

"I know. I know. I know," said Remo impatiently.

"I do not know what you do not know. Your ignorance never fails to astound me so I must be cautious in teaching you."

"I know about craps, Little Father."

"Very well. The master made a slapping motion and I lowered my head beneath it. The slap would appear fast to those untrained, but for the trained, it was slow. Then he taught me about the balance of the dice, which are really squares. And I became proficient —for they are just squares with dots, which are usually common in balance except when cheaters rearrange their balance."

Remo nodded politely.

"One day, he prepared a feast and gave me half. But before I ate, he said, 'I will game you for the whole feast. You may throw the dice,' he said. I was delighted."

"Didn't you think he might have something up his sleeve? Some sort of angle?"

"A child thinks that the world is arranged as his own personal gift. Look to your own mind, for example."

"Yes, Little Father," said Remo, almost longing for a return to the long moments of silence.

"Anyway, I threw the dice and won. But when I moved to gather the feast the master struck me.

" 'You did not win,' he said. 'Why do you gather the food?'

" 'But I won,' I said.

" 'And I say you did not win,' he said, and he slapped me again. 'I won,' I responded but he cuffed me cross the room. And he said that with the slap that I had easily avoided when he first showed me the dice, he could now hurtle me across the room. And what he told me I will never forget: 'He who cannot defend himself owns nothing, not even good fortune or his life.' And so that I would never forget, he made me watch hungry while he ate. In Sinanju, we did not waste food."

"He screwed you out of a meal, huh?" said Remo.

"He gave me many meals that night. He gave the village many meals that night. And that night, he gave you many meals too, for in my not eating, I learned how to make sure that I would always eat and that others would always eat."

"Seems like a hell of a way to make a point. Cheating a kid out of his supper."

"When a Master has someone worthwhile to teach, he teaches. When a Master must struggle with a pale piece of a pig's ear, he must tell stories."

"If tonight's the night, Little Father, and I think it is, I should be back by sunrise."

"For a fool, the sun never rises."

"I understand. I understand. I understand already. Jeez. Enough."

"More than enough for someone who does not appreciate gifts and denies little nothings in return."

At the door, Remo asked if there was anything

other than America's leading singer that Chiun would want Remo to bring him. Remo regretted asking the very minute he spoke.

"Just bring back someone who will listen."

"I thought so."

"Work on the balance tonight. Work balance into what you do. It is always good to work on balance."

"Yes, Little Father," said Remo glumly, as if he were responding to Sister Mary Francis back at the orphanage school. The motel hallway was strung with brightly colored lights, and a real Christmas tree sat on a coffee table in the lobby. Remo went out into the cold alone, hearing the twinkle of Muzak Christmas carols. It was the yuletide season. He was going to work.

The Wilberforce house was lit, but without the bright Christmas bulbs. Remo could see the tree through the living-room window, a small artificial cone of green strung with what appeared to be popcorn. Well, it was better than a bush with tennis balls. Down the street, Remo saw a house with an eight-light candelabra. Even the Jews had Hannukah. They adapted. They made a minor holiday into a major one to get into the spirit of the season and they had five thousand years, which even Chiun had to admit was something. What did Remo have? The Feast of the Pig? The Feast of the Pig and a bush with tennis balls.

A car skittered down the slushy street and the cold gray slush spattering at him reminded him who he was. He put away his anger, for a man could not work with anger, not this work and not properly. He would be angry later.

Maybe later he would kick someone's tires and wish them merry Feast of the Pig or something, but right now, while midnight approached and the carols died away as people went warm to bed, he had the only thing the Master of Sinanju told him he would ever really have. His discipline.

It was about 3 A.M. when a car without headlights parked a block away and left its motor running. Two men in dark overcoats carrying packages under their arms struggled from the car and up the street. Remo could hear the contents of their packages sloshing. Probably kerosene. He stood still in the darkness of a curbside tree and let them pass close. He smelled the alcohol on their breath and moved in behind them, two trudging figures followed by a feather-light darkness.

They crossed the street and the fragment of front footage that, in the spring, would be the Wilberforce lawn. They breathed heavily. When one quietly began to jimmy the basement window, Remo whispered:

"Merry Feast of the Pig."

"Shhhh," said the man with the jimmy.

"I didn't say nothing," said the one with the two packages.

"Merry Feast of the Pig. Fond farewells to men of good will," said Remo. "Or bad will. Or whatever."

"Hey. Who are you?" asked the man on his knees, snow up to his groin. His face was reddened and angry.

"I am the Spirit of Sinanju here to tell you you have the wrong house. This isn't the Wilberforce house."

"What you talking about?"

"You've got the wrong house. C'mon with me."

"What you doing here in just a tee-shirt? Ain't you cold? Who are you?"

"I'm the Spirit of Sinanju come to show you the right house to burn down. I help all assassins on the eve of the Feast of the Pig."

"No one's burning nothing," said the man standing.

His voice made desperate cloud puffs in the night. So surprised was he at the man before him wearing just a dark tee-shirt that he did not notice this odd stranger made no exhalation clouds when he spoke.

"You're not Santa Claus, right? Right. What are you doing here with that kerosene or whatever if it's not to torch, right? Right. So why torch the wrong place? Come with me," said Remo.

"You know this guy, Marvin?" asked the man with snow clotted to his waist.

"Never seen him," said the man with the packages.

"I am the Spirit of Sinanju come to show you the right house," said Remo. "Come with me. I'll show you the Wilberforce house."

"What you think, Marvin?"

"I think I don't know."

"I think I don't know, too."

"Should we plug him?"

"I'm a torch, not a hit man, Marvin."

"Well, see what he says. Jeez, he's a spooky looking son of a bitch, huh?"

The dark thin figure beckoned, the two men looked up, both of them less sure they were at the Wilberforce house than they had been when they trudged through the snow along the side of the house.

"See what he says. Jeez. Right, Marvin?"

"Why not? Shhh."

Across the street, the dark figure that seemed to glide across the snow beckoned for them to lend an ear. Unfortunately, he didn't want the ear as a loan. Marvin the Torch felt a searing tear at the side of his head. He went for the man with his mittened hand, but the hand did not move. He felt nothing where the glove began.

His partner swung the package at the dark figure and Marvin the Torch saw only the flashing white of a hand and heard the thump of something smacking an overcoat. Then his sidekick was flattened in the slush, face down, can out, and his legs sticking out starkly at angles that legs should not stick out from bodies.

"We celebrate the Feast of the Pig by asking questions," said Remo.

"What?" said Marvin the Torch.

"Turn your head toward the ear you have left. That's right. Now, Marvin, who sent you?"

"What happened?"

"No. On the Feast of the Pig, the Spirit of Sinanju asks the questions. Who hired you, asks the Spirit of Sinanju and you say . . . ?"

"Nick Banno. Nick. Nick Banno."

"Ahhh, a Saint Nick. And where does Nick Banno live?"

"I ain't saying no more," said Marvin the Torch. He saw the hand move, felt a sharp burning in his chest and he suddenly remembered exactly where Big Nick lived, how much he had paid, where Big Nick was spending the evening, what Big Nick looked like and that he had never liked Big Nick. Not at all.

"Good night and merry Feast of the Pig," said the weirdo stranger in the black tee-shirt and Marvin the Torch didn't even see the flashing hand. He went to sleep very quickly, forever.

Down the street, the driver of the waiting car with its lights out tried to make out what had happened to Marvin the Torch and his assistant. The snow clouded his vision. He thought he heard someone say something like "Merry Feast of the Pig" and then he heard nothing. For good.

"Deck the streets with fallen bodies, fa, la, la, la, la, la, la, la, la," sang Remo. He liked the tune so he sang louder.

A light turned on in a second-floor window and someone yelled for him to shut up.

"Merry Feast of the Pig," called out Remo.

"Goddamned drunk," came the voice from the window and in the spirit of the Feast of the Pig, Remo kicked in a tire of the closest car in the hopes that it belonged to the yeller.

The home of Nicholas Banno was a testament to bad taste and the power company. It shone in red and green and orange and yellow and blue strings of lights, hung, draped and strung over a yard filled with enough statuary to shame a Caesar.

Remo knocked.

A light went on upstairs.

There was thumping inside the house.

A portly man in a red velvet smoking jacket answered the door. He blinked his sleep-shrouded eyes open. A small handgun was in his right pocket and so was his hand, Remo saw.

"Nicholas Banno?" asked Remo pleasantly.

"Yeah. Hey, are you all right? You ain't got a coat. C'mon inside and get warm."

"Don't make my job difficult by being nice," said Remo. "You've got to get into the spirit of the Feast of the Pig. Death on earth to men of bad will," and with that, Nicholas Banno felt two light taps on his chest, saw his lawn statuary coming toward him, felt an incredible pain on the back of his neck which eased only when he said who he worked for and where the person was now. He did not hear his wife call out, asking if everything was all right.

"All's well," called out Remo. "Merry Feast of the Pig."

"Nick. Nick. Are you okay? Nick?"

Into the pre-dawn streets of Scranton Remo trotted,

the Spirit of Sinanju making its Feast of the Pig eve visits. Chiun, naturally, would not approve. But that was Chiun. And if Remo wished to make a game of work during the Christmas holidays, then that was Remo's way. Every religious discipline was affected by the nationalities that adopted it. In a way, Remo might be considered American Sinanju, Reformed Sinanju, American Rite Sinanju.

"Merry Feast of the Pig," he called out again. He saw a squad car turn away from him, apparently not wanting to pick up another drunken reveler in the cold snow that evening.

John Larimer was president of the First National Agricultural Bank and Trust Company of Scranton, a good father, a stable member of the community, at least until 2:30 A.M., according to Nick Banno, who had been very truthful. Most people were when they were in pain.

After 2:30 A.M., he stopped being a good father and a stable member of the community and began enjoying life. John Larimer had a little apartment in what for Scranton would be considered a high rise. Even the president of a bank had financial limitations, but John Larimer had a large source of very liquid and very untaxable income and when he stopped being a family man, he could enjoy his nights with Fifi, Honey, Pussy and Snookums, who were very expensive playmates.

Their game required money. Much money. Cash. John Larimer would enter the huge apartment through the kitchen door. Just outside the kitchen, in a closet, was a new wardrobe, not quite the grays and blacks he wore to work.

He hung up his suit and his vest, put away his brown cordovan shoes, white shirt and striped tie.

Then he put on his high red boots with the laces to the top, his yellow silk pants, his silk cape, his diamond-studded coke spoon and his mink safari hat. He placed diamond and ruby rings on his fingers and, but for being somewhat paunchy and in his middle fifties and a little pale, he would have been a fine figure of a pimp.

"Women. I is home," he called out, strutting into a plush, rugged living room with modern lights hanging over low, slick leather sofas.

"Sweet Johnny. Sweet Johnny," called out Honey. She came fluffing into the living room, awash in white fur and pink negligee.

"He's home. The man is home," shrieked Pussy. She trotted into the living room in pumps and thin black lace.

Sweet Johnny Larimer stood in the center of the room, sporting his arrogance, his hands on hips, his face a cold mask.

When all the women were pawing him and touching his parts and showering him with kisses, he pushed them away.

"I come for the money, not the honey. No money, no sweet Johnny." And he waited as they rushed back to their rooms to bring him cash. That the amounts they returned to him were less than a tenth of the amounts he left them in fat white envelopes each week was not a point to be mentioned. In fact, it was necessary to forget, for if someone had mentioned it, the whole game would have been ruined beyond repair. Also not mentioned was the girl who was to be called short. The girls rotated feigning the shortage of money, because sometimes it could be painful. Of course, it was necessary. The one who was to be short this night was Pussy, a peroxide blonde with big soft breasts. She smoked a cigarette in her room before returning. She avoided looking at herself in the large vanity mirror.

"Fucking idiot," she mumbled to herself about Sweet Johnny. Then, "Who's the idiot? You're getting slapped around, sweetie, not him. Then again, he's paying, not you." If she had to decide whether to stay on the nights it was her turn to be short, she told herself she would rather go back to the streets. But after it was over, she had a month before it was her turn again and it would be foolish to pass up all that good money during the easy periods. Before she knew it, it was her turn again, and afterwards she had the easy money again. And so on for a year and a half. At least she was banking the bread. It wasn't as though she had to give it to a man. And since Sweet Johnny was John Larimer, president of the bank, he had propitiously directed her toward safe, high-yield bonds.

"Someone's missing and someone's short." She heard Sweet Johnny's voice roaring.

Pussy snuffed out her cigarette in an ash tray. One of the hot sparks touched her pinkie and it hurt. She came out of her room sucking her pinkie.

"The money, woman," said Sweet Johnny.

"Here it is, precious. I had a bad week," said Pussy, offering up two tens and a five.

"This is twenty-five. You short. Doan fuck with my money, woman."

Pussy felt the sharp slap, but her pinky hurt so much she forgot to show magnified pain.

That was a mistake. John Larimer's knee came up into her belly and she doubled over. He had never kneed her before.

"Bitch. Bitch. Damned white bitch," he yelled. She felt his weight come down on her, then her wives-in-law were grabbing her wrists and holding them, so

67

she could not move. This was going to be different. This wasn't just a slapping around.

"Get your goddamned hands off me, you fucking banker. Banker. Fucking banker," yelled Pussy and she saw the sudden hatred in the other girls' faces, hatred that told her they weren't about to lose their source of income. Fifi hit her in the mouth with a lamp.

"Burn her tits, Sweet Johnny. Don't let no woman mouth you like that. You our man," said Fifi.

"Yeah, yeah," said Larimer. "That right."

"She hates burning. Burn her. Burn the bitch. You the man."

"Noooo. Please, no," said Pussy, but she felt a pillow stuffing her mouth and her negligee being ripped off and then a mouth on her breast and long hair flowing against her neck. It was one of her sisters.

"Get it hard so you burn the tip. That really hurts."

Her wives-in-law were punishing her for almost blowing the game, and their vengeance was as bad as any real pimp's.

She thought the pain would have to end, but it got worse and steeper and it was jabbing down toward her belly button and she smelled her own burning flesh mixing with the heavy stink of perfume from her wives-in-law.

When the burning pain started marching into her pubic hair, she heard a strange voice calling out a strange holiday.

"Merry Feast of the Pig, one and all."

The pain stopped marching, hands released her and she heard a swishing of air, and bones cracking. She lay on the rug, quivering in pain. She heard someone ask Larimer questions and she heard the questions being answered in a tearful voice. All of them.

"Thank you and merry Feast of the Pig."

And then she heard what sounded like a big bone popping and the pillow was gently taken from her mouth.

"Have any Vitamin E here?"

Pussy kept her eyes closed. She did not want to open them. She did not want to see. If she kept her eyes closed, it wouldn't hurt so much.

"In the bathroom," she hissed. "One of the girls uses it."

"Thank you."

She did not hear the man go to the bathroom but quickly, almost too quickly, felt liquid pouring on the pain in her upper body. Then she felt sheets wrapping her gently and she was lifted very smoothly, surprisingly very smoothly, and placed gently on something soft into which her body sank. It was a bed.

"You rest here. Every day, maybe twice a day, keep squeezing Vitamin E capsules on your burns. Guaranteed. Helps the scars heal and breathe."

"The pain. Something for the pain."

"A little hand acupuncture, my dear. We of the Regular Established Reformed American Rite of Sinanju know these things."

She felt a hand search for a point on her neck and there was a sharp sting there and then her body was numb from shoulders down.

"Thank you. Thank you. Thank you so much."

"I have a question. What's a rotten girl like you doing in a nice business like this?"

Pussy did not want to laugh, not now. Not the way she was, not here, not after the horror. But she thought the remark incredibly funny.

"The Regular Established Reformed American Rite has a sense of humor. That is where we differ from the Eastern Rite. Merry Feast of the Pig and to all a last night."

Later, at noon, when the police and the coroner's office were all over the apartment and everyone was asking her questions all at once she saw the bodies being taken out with sheets over the faces. She tried to explain what happened, but someone said she was in shock and they gave her a sedative and pain killer. It unfortunately took away the good effects of the hand acupuncture which no one believed but which had worked so well and she was again in pain and misery.

Remo left the Scranton version of the high rise. It was not quite yet dawn and he headed toward his last stop, that given him by the late John Larimer, also known as Sweet Johnny.

The Stace mansion was a magnificent three-story structure combining elements of Greek and English architecture. Its massive front had a beautiful reinforced bolt lock that popped in a nice, neat crack.

Stace, according to Larimer, was a very young-looking fifty-five with slightly graying hair and a trim, well-built body that tended to heft in the shoulders.

Remo night-silently went through the mansion checking beds but found no trim middle-fifties man with heft in the shoulders. There was a very thin man in a servant's room, a pudgy man and his pudgier wife in another servant's room, two teenagers—each in their own rooms, and an elderly man, emaciated, dried up and obviously terminal, in what appeared to be the master bedroom.

So Remo awakened the pudgy man in the servant's room who in his sudden shock said indeed Mr. Stace was the one in the master bedroom, but he had not come out of it for two days. Remo put the pudgy man back to sleep again, carefully, so that it would not be permanent.

The wizened old specter in the master bedroom

was gently awakened with a tap on his leathery forehead, and Remo led him quietly downstairs to the basement. The old man was hardly able to walk; his feet shuffled, and his eyes rolled slowly about, aimlessly, as if looking for lost youth.

"Are you Anthony Stace, alias Anselmo Stacio?" Remo asked.

The old man nodded. "It doesn't matter any more. It doesn't matter. It doesn't matter," he said. His voice cracked with age.

Remo looked at the thin white hair, the crinkling skin hanging beneath the eyes, the bony hands with the age spots, the old stoop of the spine.

"You don't look like you're in your mid-fifties," Remo said.

"That's right. I don't look it."

"Well, sorry to wake you, old fella, but you've been playing naughty-naughty. That's not always unprofitable, but if you get in the way of Upstairs, it's invariably fatal."

"What are you going to take away from me, young man? A day? A few hours? A minute? What do you want to know? It doesn't make any difference anymore."

The old man sat heavily on a crate near the boiler.

"You know, you're really spoiling the spirit of the Feast of the Pig. You sure you don't want to be a little nasty or angry? Would you like to call some of your bodyguards? Maybe threaten me?"

"It's all over. Nothing will do any good anymore. It just doesn't matter. Nothing matters."

"Well, okay. If you want to be that way about it. Go ahead, ruin the whole evening." And Remo heard about why Stace had wanted Wilberforce out of the way, the loan-shark funnel through the bank, the

71

three attempts on Wilberforce's life and how it all didn't mean much anymore.

"Anything else?"

"You have everything. Just a word of advice. Stay out of hospitals."

Was that a smile he saw on the old man's face? Remo started to find out for certain if there was anything else, but the man's age and his downed spirit seemed like a depressing armor, and since everything made sense and since there appeared to be no loose ends, nothing more to find out about, Remo said goodbye and dispatched Anselmo Stacio, alias Anthony Stace, in the basement of his mansion on the Eve of the Feast of the Pig.

And across town in the Wilberforce house, Nathan David Wilberforce woke up with one hell of a head cold.

Mrs. Wilberforce phoned a doctor.

CHAPTER SIX

Mrs. Wilberforce blamed herself. If she hadn't been so lax with Nathan David . . . if she had insisted that he wear his rubbers . . . gone to the office to make sure . . . it was those lunch hours that did it. A person could walk out willy nilly in the snow in his bare feet even and what would the government care? She could see why there were so many radicals nowadays. Government insensitivity.

"It's more than rubbers," said the doctor gravely. He spoke in hushed tones outside Nathan David's room. "It's pneumonia. We'll have to hospitalize him immediately."

"I'll break the news," said Mrs. Wilberforce.

The doctor nodded and asked for a phone. He had called it pneumonia. Most of the symptoms were pneumonia. And why the hell not pneumonia? It was probably pneumonia, and when the patient got to the hospital, they could run more tests and make sure it was pneumonia or whatever. There was trouble in the lungs and the man had to be in the hospital so they might be able to control whatever he had or at least get some handle on it.

You couldn't tell the next of kin you didn't know. That caused panic. You had to give them something to hold on to, something they knew could be cured. If it turned out to be incurable, well, let a specialist handle that. He wasn't being paid enough money for a Christmas season house call to tell someone he didn't know what was wrong with a patient . . . that it could be terminal. Then again, it was very possible, even probable, that it wasn't terminal.

The human body was a miraculous thing. It healed itself in so many ways. And if it did, then he would have saved the patient and he would be a hero. He phoned the hospital where he had privileges, fought for and got a bed. No, he couldn't wait another day. He had a sick patient, he told the admitting office. Pneumonia.

He apologized for being unable to wait for the ambulance and Mrs. Wilberforce tearfully accepted his apologies.

"Other house calls. We're so busy."

"Yes, I know. It's a hard life, being a doctor," said Mrs. Wilberforce, and watched him put on his cashmere coat and carefully cross the unshoveled walk to his black Eldorado Cadillac with the high antenna.

By nightfall, there were complications and by dawn a special team of physicians was called in to save Nathan David's life. They worked through noon. Mrs. Wilberforce was called into a private office. She was introduced to one of the visiting doctors, a kindly looking man with a drawn aquiline face.

"We did everything we could," said the doctor.

"Complications?" asked Mrs. Wilberforce.

"Yes. Complications," said Dr. Daniel Demmet.

Remo was surprised to see Dr. Harold Smith travel all the way out to California to congratulate him for a job well done. Remo and Chiun had been in a La Jolla waterfront hotel suite for two days, having traveled on Sunday, when Chiun said none of the good dramas were on television, just many fat men running into each other. The Master of Sinanju had written the networks suggesting that it would be a far nicer way to celebrate Sundays and national holidays by having fine daytime drama than all that running into each other and fat men hurting each other ineptly. Each network had answered, thanking him for his interest in their programming. Assuming they were asking for guidance, Chiun had responded by outlining how each could improve its shows by taking off violence and shooting and fat people running into each other and other people sitting down and just talking. They could run their daytime dramas from sunrise to sunset and invigorate the minds of the populace with beauty. Again, Chiun had received letters thanking him for his help, at a post office box set up for him by Upstairs in a northeastern state.

Chiun was delighted. To him, this meant that there would be seven full days a week of what Remo called soap operas and they would never be cancelled for fat men running into each other. But as each Sunday came and passed, Chiun became more disappointed, damning the networks as liars who should be shown what beauty was. Remo decided it would be wise to explain to Chiun that the network executives were really friends of the emperor, which was the only thing Chiun could understand as a reason for not fatally visiting beauty upon the network executives who had lied to him. Chiun finally resigned himself to what he called American craziness.

But now the soaps were on again and Remo quietly led Smith to a sitting room where they could talk. Smith carried his briefcase and wore an unseasonably heavy coat—unseasonable for La Jolla at noon.

"It was nothing," said Remo. "A piece of cake. I

jumped the pipe to the source and got the source. You got the whole report the morning after."

"I see," said Smith. He unlocked the briefcase and sorted out three typewritten sheets. They were of translucent material that when placed over each other in the correct fashion formed understandable writing, or at least to Smith. Remo couldn't make out the writing. It appeared like notes.

"There were a few problems and I want to get them ironed out. How many people were in the pipeline you jumped?"

"I don't know. Let's see, one, two, three, uh, four, the fat guy with the statues, six with the guy with the penthouse, the broads, three, I think, and uh, the source, so that's eight. Eight," said Remo.

"They were all necessary?"

"Yeah. Sure. It's not entertainment. I don't go around doing someone because I don't like him."

"I see. And did you possibly go through Scranton wishing Merry Pig or something? We're getting some very strange stories about that night. The city is in a state of terror, which was not exactly your purpose or the purpose of our organization."

"Oh, that," said Remo smiling. "The Feast of the Pig. It's sort of an inside joke I have with myself."

"Well, it seems as if you shared it quite freely that night."

Remo shrugged.

"I thought you were well aware of our mission. If this becomes known, the entire purpose of our organization is for naught. The government, everything. Remo, you don't understand the gravity of this. We're struggling to keep a country alive."

"And if it doesn't want to stay alive, Smitty?"

"Are you beginning to think like Chiun that one emperor is the same as another? That the only thing important is the House of Sinanju? I know how Chiun thinks."

"Chiun's worth his money. You have no complaints. Chiun's worth more than his money. He didn't leave himself and the organization as open as a meadow once.* You know, Smitty, I mean, let's look at this thing. Let's really look at it. Sinanju has got a hell of a lot more going for it than any little three-hundred-year-old country."

"I wasn't complaining about Chiun, Remo. Chiun is Chiun. But you, what about you? Where are your loyalties?"

"With myself. And if you don't like it, we can end this thing. You may not know it, but I am incredibly employable. Chiun keeps getting job offers at the post office box."

"I know that, Remo. I have the mail read. But where do you stand?"

"I do my frigging job."

"Then do it. Wilberforce is dead."

"How can he be dead?"

"When the heart stops, when the brain stops functioning, when a person no longer breathes, he is dead, Remo. That is what we, even in a little three-hundred-year-old country, call dead."

"Who got him?"

"Pneumonia with complications."

Remo rose from the chair and bowed deeply. "My apologies for once again having failed you. Next time I will guard his lungs with my life."

"It was your job to keep him alive."

"I thought we already established this. I can do what I can do. I can do no more. You want to save

*Destroyer #14, *Judgment Day*.

someone from pneumonia, get yourself a nurse or a doctor. You don't need me."

"We did an autopsy on Wilberforce. Surreptitiously, of course. It's possible he was killed on the operating table."

"Then get better doctors. What do you want from me?"

"I want you, without wreaking havoc and slaughter indiscriminately, to find out which doctors may be killers. It is beyond coincidence. The law of probabilities says these people are being killed."

"Good thing we have math. Now we know for sure Wilberforce is dead."

"We know more than that," said Smith. "We're almost sure there's a medical system that has become a killer. I have here a list of doctors to check. I do not under any circumstances want indiscriminate killing. I don't want to have to deal with another Scranton."

"So you won't have another Scranton, sweetheart. Don't get so angry."

"I am not angry. I am sad. I am sad to see what is happening to you. There is something good in this country. It is a hope that the world needs now. And if you or others do not believe it, nevertheless this hope exists and I wanted very much for you to share it, too."

Remo was silent. He heard the traffic down on the street, heard the air conditioner hum and felt uneasy.

"Yeah. Well," said Remo, "I don't believe in talking about it."

"All right," said Smith. "I understand."

When the five-minute newsbreak came just before one o'clock, Chiun glided into the room in which Remo and Smith were going over the probables on the list of doctors. They had pinpointed an exclusive medical clinic outside of Baltimore, a clinic frequented by many high government officials.

"Why did you not tell me Dr. Smith was here?" demanded Chiun angrily. "When I heard voices, I thought, no, it could not be Dr. Smith for surely Remo would tell me of such an important visit. I did not even entertain the possible thought that Dr. Smith could be here and I would not be informed."

Chiun bowed graciously and Smith returned it with a short nod.

"It's all right. We have everything worked out."

"I overheard there were possible improprieties," said Chiun and for four and a half minutes, Chiun vowed the services of the House of Sinanju to Emperor Smith, called perfection of service to Emperor Smith the goal of the House of Sinanju, hinted darkly that there were forces in Smith's empire that wished him no good and the House of Sinanju was here to assure him that he need but point them out and he would have no further worries. Approximately four seconds before the next soap opera was to come on, Chiun vowed service to the death and was out of the room before Smith could respond.

"He's got a certain grace," said Smith.

"Yeah, grace," said Remo.

When Smith was gone and when the organ music followed Dr. Ravenel's last worry about Marcia Mason's failing to appear at Dorothy's Dunsmore's cocktail party because her unwed daughter might be pregnant with a child of Rad Dexter's leprosy-ridden son, Remo spoke to Chiun.

"Little Father, why did you give Smith all that nonsense?"

"An emperor wants nonsense. You were telling him the truth, were you not?"

"Yeah. How did you know?"

"I heard his annoyance. No emperor wants the truth for the very fact of a man being an emperor is a lie unto itself. What would you tell a khan or a czar or prince? That he rules because of his extraordinary skill in choosing his parents? Hah. They are born with lies and they spend their lives seeking facts to support those lies. Therefore a fact supporting a lie must be a lie itself, and therefore when you deal with an emperor you must, above all, avoid getting too close to the truth. That was why Smith was annoyed."

"We don't have emperors like that in America. People are chosen by merit and elections."

"Of elections, millions vote, do they not?"

"Yeah. Millions."

"Do these millions ever sit down and talk with the man they vote for?"

"Well, no, of course not. But they hear him speak."

"And do they have the opportunity to say what did you mean by this and what did you mean by that and why do you say this now when you said that yesterday?"

"Reporters question them."

"Then only reporters should vote."

"What about merit?" asked Remo. He crossed his arms.

"The biggest lie of all which requires the most fantastic fabrications to support it. Should a man be chosen by this merit, then everything he does must be meritorious. Since this is impossible, especially if one is not born in Sinanju, one must create lies to show that he is always meritorious. In the future, you would do well to tell Smith the lie he wishes to hear."

"And what lie would that be, Little Father?"

"That you love America and that one form of government is better than another."

There was silence in the hotel suite, as Remo pondered Chiun's statement. That the second was a lie, he did not doubt. But love America? Perhaps, after all, he really did. It would be a thing Chiun could not understand.

The silence was broken by Chiun muttering. It was a familiar phrase, referring to the inability of even the Master of Sinanju to transform mud into diamonds.

CHAPTER SEVEN

Ms. Kathleen Hahl made time on her busy schedule to see one visitor who didn't want to see her.

"I want to see the administrator of the Robler Clinic, not the assistant administrator. What's your name, young lady? And don't beat around the bush. I've been given more information that made less sense in the last two days than since I don't know when," said Mrs. Wilberforce.

"Won't you please sit down?"

"I'll stand, thank you. I don't intend to stay here long."

"If you sit down, I can talk to you," said the snippet of a girl with the brownish red hair and the loose white blouse that hid who knew what sort of lewd contraption of a bra instead of a solid, sensible, firm, snug, strong and holding underwear as God had intended bras to be. If there was one fortunate thing in this whole unfortunate tragedy, it was that girls like this would no longer be looking to defile Nathan David.

When Mrs. Wilberforce thought about Nathan David she became deeply sad and almost instantly angry. Furious.

"My name is Ms. Hahl. Won't you sit down, please? I'd like to help you."

"Good. Then I want to see every doctor who treated Nathan David Wilberforce. I know they came from this clinic. I have their names right here. Right here in my pocketbook."

"This Mr. Wilberforce is a patient here, is that right?"

"He is not. He is dead. I gave your doctors a healthy boy and they gave me back a corpse. You murdered him. Murder." And seeing that this word somehow disturbed the young woman, Mrs. Wilberforce yelled the word full lung. "Murder. Murder. Murder. A hospital of murderers."

"Mrs. Wilberforce, please. How can I help you? What do you want?"

"Admit you're a pack of murderers. Admit it. Have your doctors admit it. They had to import doctors to kill Nathan David. The local doctors weren't good enough. I spoke to my lawyer. I know. You doctors stick together. But you're not fooling me. I gave them a healthy boy who wore his rubbers—he wore them, I checked. He put on his rubbers and I gave him his vitamins and you killed him. That's what you did. Dead. Murdered. A whole hospital of murderers."

"Mrs. Wilberforce, now you know that is not true," Ms. Hahl said. Her voice was sincere, yet gentle, yet very firm.

"I don't know it's not true unless you prove it to me. Until I see those murderers investigated and brought up on charges. You have just one decent doctor in your entire hospital, and he's just the anesthesiologist. If he were the surgeon, Nathan David would be alive today."

"Dr. Demmet?"

"Yes. Him. He was decent. He showed proper concern. He was as heartbroken as I was. If all doctors were like Dr. Demmet, Nathan David would be alive today. He was the only one who spoke to me. The others just hung their heads and walked away, but not Dr. Demmet." Mrs. Wilberforce began to sob. She felt a soft arm on her shoulder. It was the girl.

"Most men can be so insensitive. They don't know feelings," said Ms. Hahl.

Mrs. Wilberforce felt a strange exciting tingle overcome her body, but she suppressed it as she had suppressed all those things all her life. She wasn't about to begin now.

"I want an investigation or I will . . . I will . . . I will print thousands of cards saying the Robler Clinic is a hotbed of murderers and mail them to every official everywhere."

"You know that's not so, Mrs. Wilberforce," said Ms. Hahl. Her hand moved to the big woman's shoulder and as it began to descend down toward the massive Wilberforce bosom, she felt a light slap on her wrist.

"I don't like touching," said Mrs. Wilberforce.

"I'm sorry. I didn't realize."

"That's all right. What are you going to do?"

"I'll have an investigation. I'll have Dr. Demmet do it, but you've got to do something, Mrs. Wilberforce. You've got to help me. I need your help."

"Don't stand so close. It makes me nervous."

"You've got to keep this investigation very very quiet. Very quiet. Because you know how doctors are. If they suspect that we're having an investigation, then they'll become very defensive."

"Then you agree with me? Nathan David was . . . please, stop that with the hands . . . you agree that they killed Nathan David. Medical malpractice."

"No, I don't. I honestly don't agree with you. But

I want you to see for yourself. You're a grieved mother and I want you to see exactly what happened."

Mrs. Wilberforce brushed a nasty intruding hand away from her lap and stood up firmly.

"All right. But if I don't receive satisfaction, I will insist upon seeing the director and then out go the cards with the accusations."

"Agreed," said Ms. Hahl. "Are you staying in town?"

"Close by. In Baltimore."

"Watch yourself on the streets there. The streets are dangerous."

"I don't go out at night and I don't carouse. I have no need to worry."

"You're right. You're so sweet. May I kiss you?"

"No. No. Of course not."

"You remind me of my mother. Just a daughterly kiss."

"No. Definitely not," said Mrs. Wilberforce, and she was out of the office stamping down the hallway.

Kathy Hahl went back to her desk.

"Shit," she said and tapped a pencil briefly on a small stack of silver tablets noting leadership of the Robler Clinic annual fund. She reached into a center desk drawer, withdrew an ornate golden ring and toyed with it as she dialed Dr. Demmet's office. He wasn't there. She dialed his home. He wasn't there. She dialed the Fair Oaks Country Club and got him, noting to herself that that was where she should have tried in the first place. He was on call that day should have left a telephone number where he could be reached. He hadn't.

"Hi, Dan. This is Kathy. How are you, sweetie?"

"No," said Dr. Demmet.

"No is the way you are?"

"Whatever you want, the answer is negative."

"I don't want anything from you, Dan, except your money."

"You're not getting me into a three stroke a side game in winter golf."

"A half stroke a hole, Dan. That's four and a half a side."

"You'd never give me that."

"I'm giving it to you, Dan. You're just a bad golfer, Dan. You choke. You're a loser, Dan. Haven't you realized that by now?" Her voice was silky contempt.

"I'm not taking these insults for a hundred dollars a side."

"You name your price, Danny Boy. The bigger it is, the faster you'll choke."

"What are you up to, Kathy? What do you want?"

"I'm coming right out to the club."

Kathy Hahl hung up the phone mid-chatter. She told her secretary she would not be back that day and drove out to the Fair Oaks Country Club, making note of the weather. The snow had yet to stick so they would not have to use the red balls. The ground was probably ice hard from the snow that melted in the Maryland sun and then froze again in the Maryland night. They hadn't had much sun for the last three days. With an ice-hard course, the whole game was control. Demmet had one advantage. His man's strength. But if he tried to use it, Kathy Hahl knew she could give him a stroke a hole, maybe even one and a half, and win handily.

She had spent a young lifetime beating men. She had to. They were the only ones around worth beating. They had the money. Like fund raising. If there was one last reluctant vestige of medieval male chauvinism, it was fund raising. Women just weren't allowed. Oh, there were the usual excuses, how people didn't trust women, especially young women with large sums of money, how the corporate world would not respond to a woman running a fund-raising operation, how, well, it just wasn't done.

Because of Robler's reputation as a socially progressive institution, she had applied for a job there and been hired as an associate director of program development. There were articles and pictures and questions about how it felt to be the first female. It was all very impressive except that associate director in fund raising really meant only one thing. They gave you a title so that people wouldn't think they were being insulted speaking to a nobody. This held true for the men, too. For a woman, though, it meant additionally that she typed, filed, counted numbers and made sure that the male associate directors got their coffee.

This, for one of the first female graduates of Yale. She could always have taken woman's traditional route to wealth, traveling on her back. There were those marriage offers. Good ones. But the men were lousy lovers and besides she liked an occasional girl also. Anyway, why should she, because of a backward social system, in essence have to peddle her ass for a living?

Like most people who engage in multiple murder, she could claim some justice on her side. All it needed was a vehicle. She had played golf regularly with Dr. Demmet to supplement her associate director's salary, which was, naturally, lower than that of a male associate director. Demmet told her about the operating room. Tales of surgeons coming in so depressed by Quaalude that they had to be helped from the operating table. The special nurse who had to make sure the tools of the trade weren't left inside the patient. She learned a new word: *iatrogenics*. It referred to the patients killed by the usual mess and mistake in a hopsital, rather than by any individual case of malpractice.

Oh, but it was hard to pin down. Doctors were not stupid. Gross incompetence would get them outside review boards. And so hospitals always tidied their own houses and this gave those in the profession moral support in never testifying against another doctor. It occurred to her that a doctor could safely kill anyone he chose and, short of spitting into a surgical incision, never be criticized.

Then came that first bequest. It was accidental. No one else was in the office. She responded on the telephone. A leading member of the community wanted to leave her fortune to the Robler Clinic where she knew her money would do some good.

Kathy Hahl went to visit the woman, an aging bore whom the world would little miss and never remember. The woman had decided that the grandson who was now named in her will was a wastrel. He shouldn't get more than sustenance. Kathy Hahl told the old biddy just what she wanted to hear. That she was absolutely right.

And then Kathy Hahl saw the grandson. She had seen people spaced out before, but this boy with the flaming orange Afro hair would need a good month of detoxification to be spaced out. He had a checking account into which Grandma put $150 a week. Grandma also paid the rent, gas and electricity, and made sure food was delivered daily. About midweek, when he had gone through his allowance, he would sell the food for drugs. Kathy said she thought the culture was oppressing him. Drugs were really so cheap. Why, she could bring them to him for nothing. She did. She also got him to sign an undated statement and a little check. He said he didn't mind. All the check could be good for was $150 a week anyhow, so any check bigger than that would just bounce.

Kathy knew it was a peculiarity of the fund-raising business that someone getting a $500,000 bequest was less respected that someone bringing in $10,000 cash, the assumption being that bequests came by themselves but cash had to be promoted.

By then, Dr. Demmet was heavily in her debt, and, as she found out, heavily in debt to many of the Baltimore bookies. Kathy had just the way he could clear those debts. Demmet first called the plan absurd. Kathy said it wasn't a plan, it was a wild idea that she didn't really believe in herself.

She wondered out loud how long the old biddy might live without any external harm coming to her. Then she noted out loud how awful the old woman was. Then she got Demmet into a side bet with a bookie known to have an affinity for breaking arms when hands did not hold the cash he thought was due him.

The old lady went on the operating table at the first heavy sniffle, leaving her money not to Robler— the new will had been delayed—but to her grandson, who was told by his own lawyers that they were surprised he had made such a large contribution to the Robler Clinic. He didn't remember doing so. They showed him the statement with a current date and the huge check with a current date and his response was:

"Heavy, man."

With one more large grant, the directors of Robler Clinic saw in Ms. Hahl their new director of program development. Another Robler first. The first woman to head a fund-raising department. With judicious use of Demmet and more and more money coming in under her control, Kathy Hahl became the real power at the hospital. The next step was assistant administrator as well as chief fund-raiser.

She was on her way up and she was still able to go to bed with anyone she wanted to.

And then came the decision that seemed so clear and simple she wondered why she had not made it much easier. If people could die and leave money to Robler, they could also die and make money for her.

She suspected that she might have to recruit more doctors, but it turned out that just Demmet was enough. He was by far the best anesthesiologist in the area, and could work on any operation he chose. Step by step, he became the medical button man for Kathy Hahl's contract-killing service.

The whole life-and-death idea gave her a feeling of power. And then she discovered something about power that very few know, because they are not in a position to feel it. Power is a narcotic. You start out liking it and then you need it.

That was when Kathy Hahl realized that all the government officials who used the Robler Clinic might somehow be used to help build Kathy's power and wealth. And then that scruffy old lesbian researcher on the fifth floor had made a strange discovery, and while it was still being tested, if it held true, it could wind up giving Kathy greater power than she had ever even dreamed of.

Today Demmet would have to give that discovery another test.

Demmet was waiting in the club bar sipping a light wine. He wore a loose-fitting but warm beige jacket, red cashmere slacks and tartan golf shoes.

"You decided the stakes yet, Dan?" asked Kathy. But she already knew. If Demmet were drinking only light wine, it was going to be a heavy bet. He only drank liquor before unimportant matches.

"Four and a half strokes a side?"

"I said it."

"Why don't we make the match for everything I owe you. Everything. Double or nothing."

"That would mean you'd owe me double what you already can't pay."

"I can do more specials for you."

"There's a limit to those, Dan. Even for the Robler Clinic. It's not like we're running a supermarket for murder."

"Sometimes you act like you are," Demmet said. "For instance, Wilberforce. What was that all about? I understand the man who wanted him removed refused to pay the price?"

"That's right," said Kathy Hahl. "But the man who wanted Wilberforce removed is dead. I didn't want the authorities to look too closely at his death, and they would have if Wilberforce had continued his tax investigation. So Wilberforce had to go, too."

"You mean, we're not getting paid for Wilberforce?" Kathy nodded.

"Well, I did my job. I'm getting paid," Demmet said.

"All right, fine. Now you only owe me half of what you can't pay."

"Why are you hustling me? I know you're hustling me," Demmet said.

"All you owe against a favor, Dan."

"I'm not going to gun down someone in the streets."

"You won't have to kill a soul."

"I don't like it."

Kathy signaled the dozing bartender at the other end of the club bar.

"Two martinis, very dry. One on the rocks and straight up for me," she said to the bartender.

"What are you doing?" Demmet asked.

"I'm ordering us drinks. We're going to play for fun, right?"

"It's another hustle. I know it. I know you, Kathy. You're still hustling me."

"He doesn't want a twist. He likes a green olive. That's right. Green olive in the dry martini on the rocks. Right. Good."

"You're not suckering me into a blind bet, Kathy."

The martinis came, glistening clear, their glasses perspiring their coolness on the outside. Kathy Hahl lifted hers and sipped. It was dry and shivery and sent that good feeling through her bloodstream.

"To your health."

Demmet held his without drinking.

"You're afraid to give me that four and a half strokes a side and you're backing out."

"No. Drink up. Go ahead."

"You're a sly one, Kathy. A sly one. But do you know something, you're also stupid. You're very stupid, Kathy. You're a fool if you want to know the truth. You could have had the whole kit and kaboodle without . . ."

"Shhhh."

"I wasn't going to say anything wrong. You could have had everything with no risks. All you had to do was become Mrs. Daniel Demmet."

Kathy Hahl laughed in her drink, spurting the drink up around the edges. She wiped the bar with a cocktail napkin. She was still laughing.

"I'm sorry, Dan. I didn't mean to laugh."

"All right. Four and a half strokes a side, bitch," said Demmet and he splashed his drink into her face. But she was still laughing on the first tee.

"Your honor, Dan. I don't have the strength yet to tee off," she said, balancing herself on her driver, her face a cherry crimson, her eyes hysterical little slits. "Don't hit it too hard, this is not a day to blast it."

Dr. Daniel Demmet teed his ball and planted his feet, a generator of rage connected to a driver. He would smack this ball down the gullet of the fairway, farther than any laughing woman could reach. He would destroy her on this first hole. He would break her on this first hole. He would tempt the danger of the hardened fairways and use it to his own power. He could eagle this hole with luck, with a great hardened running fairway.

Back went the club slowly, his body coiling, down again through his left side, inside out, and pronate the wrists on contact and follow through. The ball streaked out, low at first, then soaring. At its apex it began to curve slightly right, a slice. It hit the fairway well, but the slice on the ball sent it skittering off through the rough into the leaf-laden woods. He would never find it.

He teed up again quickly, and trying to bury the memory of the disastrous slice as quickly as possible, swung with a fast back stroke, a stroke to get the shot over with. He didn't slice into the trees this time; he hit the ball directly into them. He trotted back to the golf cart he was sharing with Kathy Hahl, took three balls from his bag, ran back up to the tee, concentrated on not pushing the ball to the right again, and shanked it, spinning to the right. Only his failure to hit the ball solidly kept it in play.

"You're lying five," said Kathy and went up to the first tee. She wiggled her hips. She took a practice swing, then stepped away from the ball, breathed deeply and took another practice swing. Then she dug in, jiggled the club before the ball, and with a very slow backswing hit a small looping piddling drive one hundred and twenty yards up the fairway.

It stayed on the fairway and gained a healthy eighty-five yards on the forward roll.

"C'mon, c'mon. C'mon. You going to wait all day on the tee?" yelled Demmet. "What the hell did you use on that?"

"I finessed a five wood."

"You used a five wood off the damned tee on a four hundred and thirty-five-yard hole?"

"I'll play my game, Dan."

Four strokes behind, Demmet knew he had to do something dramatic. Since the rough was icy and since the ball was resting high up on a clump of frozen grass, he announced to Kathy he was going to use his driver and why didn't she watch? She did. So did Demmet. Playing dramatic catch-up golf, Demmet smacked the ball low and straight. It landed with stiff spit on it. The ball bounced and sped along toward the green. It was like driving on ice. It didn't stop until it had traveled three hundred and eighty yards. Demmet looked triumphantly at Kathy Hahl, her face reddening in the chill winter afternoon.

"Well?" he said.

"Well, pretty good," said Kathy Hahl, whose next shot lay up fifty yards short of the green. She chipped on for her third shot. Demmet, off to the side, tried a high dramatic pitch shot, but golf balls do not bite on frozen greens. The ball bounced off the green. By the second tee, even with the handicap, he was done. By the third tee, he was down six strokes. By the fourth, seven. By the fifth, he gave up on the first nine and suggested they cut across the fairway to the tenth hole. They were alone on the golf course.

As they drove their electric car down a tree-shrouded path, Kathy kicked his foot off the accelerator pedal. The cart stopped.

"Dan, you know you're not going to beat me."

"We'll see. We'll see. C'mon. It's cold out here."

"The best you can do now is tie me and you're not even going to do that." She let her gloved hand rest on his slacks. "Now I want something from you, Dan, and I'll be willing to even out for it, okay? I don't want you to go unpaid. I don't want to take anything away from you." She kissed his earlobe. It was red with chill.

"What do you want?" he asked.

"I want you to get Mrs. Wilberforce off my back."

"Okay. I'll do another special."

"We can't. We've done too many already. And her coming on the heels of her son might be just too much. We've got a good thing going. We don't want to spoil it." Her voice was silky smooth. "Besides," she said.

"Besides what?"

"Besides. I want to try something new on Mrs. Wilberforce."

"Like what?"

"Well, it's a special drug."

"Give it to her yourself. Put it in her prune juice."

"I tried, Dan. But I can't get close to her. It's got to be injected during a period of high excitement, if it is to work effectively in a small dosage. If the blood isn't coursing through the veins, it takes too long, and she might be found too soon."

"What kind of high excitement?" Demmet asked.

Kathy moved a hand over the front of his trousers.

"This kind of high excitement," she said.

"Oh, I see. And you want me to deliver it?"

"Yes."

"How can I? You've seen Mrs. Wilberforce. It'd be like screwing a tank."

"Don't think of her. Think of me while you're doing it. Think of this," said Kathy Hahl, unzipping his fly

05

and lowering her head, leaning over in the golf cart as their warmed bodies sent little puffs of moisture up into the leaking pines above them.

Later, Demmet asked Kathy what kind of "special drug" he was to use.

"That's my price for winning today, Dan. You don't ask."

He shrugged. It didn't really matter.

He saw Mrs. Wilberforce that night at her motel room to discuss her son's operation again. He tried thinking of Kathy Hahl's warm mouth back on the golf course, but combining the thought of Kathy and Mrs. Wilberforce sent him retching to the bathroom. In the bathroom, he cleaned up his face, and withdrew from his pocket the special ring Kathy had given him to use. He slipped it on his finger, and turned to the door, beyond which Mrs. Wilberforce waited.

Perhaps it might be easier to just throw her off a cliff.

CHAPTER EIGHT

The lobby of the Robler Clinic was three stories high. All three stories were filled with a Christmas tree, a massive thirty-foot-tall fir, decorated with multi-colored lights and thin glass balls, and festooned with red felt stockings with white names on them.

It was the first thing seen by the two men who entered the lobby through the heavy revolving doors. They paused just inside the doors.

"Ptahhhh," spat the old man, a wizened tiny Oriental who, despite the late December cold, wore only a blue robe.

"Stop it, Chiun," said the man next to him. He was apparently a young man, but his face was obscured by almost black sunglasses. The collar of his overcoat was pulled up around his ears and the lower part of his face was obscured by a white silk scarf. The elderly Oriental held him by the right elbow as if to help support him.

"Ptahhhh," Chiun spat again. "Look at it. You Westerners have a way of taking anything and turning it into garbage. How can a tree be ugly? Easy. Give it to a white man to beautify."

"Chiun," Remo said, his voice muffled by the silk

scarf. "There's the reception desk over there. Just check us in. And remember who we are."

"I would gladly abandon my knowledge of our identities, if with it I could discard my memories of that monstrosity."

Remo sighed. "Just check us in." He walked toward a row of leather couches and sat waiting.

A uniformed security guard sat behind the desk, doing double duty as receptionist and switchboard operator.

He looked up at the old Oriental standing at the high counter, his face barely visible above its top.

"Yes?" he said.

"Merry Christmas," Chiun said.

"Merry Christmas?"

"Yes. I thought I would bring holiday cheer into your life. Do you like that tree?" he asked, pointing over his shoulder but not deigning to turn around.

"We have one every year," the guard said.

"That is a non-answer to a perfectly good question," Chiun said. "Do you like the tree?"

"I guess so," the guard shrugged. "I never really look at it."

"Save yourself the trouble. Do not look at it."

"Do you have something to do with Christmas trees?" the guard asked.

"No," Chiun said. "I am Doctor Park. A room is ready for my patient, Mr. Williams. What room is it?"

"Oh, yes," the guard said, sitting up straighter on his backless, high-legged wooden stool. "You're in the new wing. Suite 515." His voice conveyed a new respect—while he had no idea who Mr. Williams was, or who this old man in front of him was, he had been cautioned right from the assistant administrator's office that a very important patient named Williams

98

was coming and he should extend all courtesies. And that meant all courtesies.

"How do we find it?" Chiun asked.

"I'll take you there." The guard rose to his feet.

"That is not necessary. Just point."

"That corridor there. Take it to the end. That's the new wing. Take the elevator to five."

"Thank you," Chiun said.

"Doctor?" the guard said, still standing.

Chiun nodded to indicate he was listening.

"Aren't you cold?"

"Cold?"

"With just that robe on?"

"Why should I be cold? Is your furnace broken?"

"I mean outdoors. It's only fifteen out."

"Sixteen," Chiun said.

"Same thing," the guard said. "Weren't you cold?"

"I am never cold when it is sixteen out. Remember. Do not look at that tree."

He walked away from the guard who scratched his head, looked at the tree, then scratched his head again.

"How'd we make out?" Remo asked when Chiun stood in front of him.

"Fine. We are in Suite 515. But we must be careful not to catch a cold. I think their furnace is broken."

"It feels warm enough in here," Remo said.

"I know. But it's only sixteen outside."

"It felt like fifteen, Little Father."

"Why don't you talk to the guard? You can compare notes on your favorite subjects: ugly trees and incorrect temperature readings."

"Take me to my room," Remo said. "I am sick and ailing and I fain would lie doon."

"Is this a joke?"

"Take me to my room."

In recognition of the $275 a day it was costing, Remo's suite was bright and cheery, with windows along two walls of the spacious living room, and soft muted lamps in the single bedroom. In place of the normal retch green to be found on hospital walls, the rooms were papered in a light sunshine-yellow flowered pattern.

The suite was also decorated with a small plastic Christmas tree atop a walnut liquor cabinet and by two highly ornamental blonde nurses.

"Mr. Williams," one said as Remo entered the room. "I'm Miss Baines and this is Miss Marshall. We're here to help make your stay pleasant."

Remo started to speak, but Chiun scooted around in front of him, imperiously waved his robed arm toward the door, and said, "Begone."

"Begone?" Miss Baines asked.

"I am Doctor Park. If we need you we will call you."

The nurse smiled uncomfortably, but she and Miss Marshall left the room.

"You didn't have to be so bossy," Remo said after they left.

"It is my understanding that this is the way doctors act," Chiun said. He looked around. "What do you think of this room?"

"Better than some motels we've been in."

"One thing disturbs its symmetry."

Remo raised an eyebrow in a question.

"This," Chiun said. He scooped the small plastic Christmas tree from the walnut cabinet. Holding it at arm's length as if to insure that it would not contaminate him by untoward proximity, he carried it to a closet, dropped it inside and closed the door tightly.

"There. That's better."

"You shouldn't have done that, Chiun. You could have redecorated with tennis balls."

"Redecorated it so that you can again refuse me a promised gift?"

"Promised, Little Father?" asked Remo, who could remember no such promise involving slavery for Barbra Streisand.

"In the eyes of a just man, a thing that should be done is a promise to the world and to himself. It separates just men from pale pieces of pigs' ears."

"Right, Chiun, right, right, right." Remo tried to change the subject. "You are clear on our plan?"

"Yes, I am clear on the plan, but it insults me to call it 'our' plan. It is your plan. You are Mr. Williams, a man of great wealth. I am your physician. We will try to find something suspicious in the hospital. You will let people know you have tax problems, and hope that someone approaches you."

"You've got it."

"I am gratified that you have shared your wisdom with me."

"You know why we're doing it this way, don't you. Chiun?"

"Yes. Because you are stupid."

"No. Because this time, we're going to be smart. In Scranton, I did everything your way. I jumped the line and hit the top. It was beautiful. Except the guy I was supposed to protect was killed. I eliminated seven or eight or something people and it didn't do a damned bit of good."

"That was my way?" Chiun asked. "To gambol about like an intoxicated soldier, wishing people 'Merry Feast of the Pig,' and strewing the landscape with corpses? No. My way is to eliminate the person who is causing the trouble. Play games with as many people as you want but if you do not get the right

101

person, you will have accomplished nothing. Do not blame on me your inability to identify the correct target. I am after all only a poor servant who is not permitted to know the secrets of you and Doctor Smith."

"Well, this time we're going to find out just who's responsible before we go off smacking anyone down."

"And to do this, it is necessary for us to play acting games as a doctor and patient?"

"Sure, Chiun. That's the beauty. With our money, we'll have free run of the hospital. No one'll interfere with someone who sent in twenty-five thousand dollars, cash in advance."

"That is much money?"

"Very much," said Remo, "even for a hospital. It might last as long as two weeks if you don't have Blue Cross and Blue Shield."

"I reserve my judgment on your plan."

"It'll work like a charm," Remo said. "No more violence."

CHAPTER NINE

Dr. Daniel Demmet walked into the office, tossed the gold ring casually on the desk, poured himself a glass of vodka from the liquor cabinet, then sat in a soft leather chair, staring sullenly at the vodka, before raising it to his lips and gurgling half of it down.

"Little early in the day for you, isn't it?" said Kathy Hahl from across the large glass-topped desk in her office.

"It's good any time of day." Demmet's voice had a tear in it, a self-pitying whine.

"Not for a doctor, though," she said.

"For the kind of doctor I am, it's perfectly acceptable," he said.

"Is that what's bugging you?"

"Yes. If you must know, I'm getting tired of all this."

"You're just upset because Mrs. Wilberforce didn't turn you on." Kathy Hahl smiled.

"Yeah," he said. "That's part of it, maybe. What was that ring business anyway?"

"Just research," Kathy Hahl said. "Something new I'm trying. Nothing for you to worry about."

103

"Will she die?" Demmet asked. He drained the rest of his vodka.

"Of course," Kathy Hahl said. "We couldn't very well let her live, could we? Not with her running around shooting her mouth off about how we did in her sweet young son."

"Well, I don't like it anymore."

"Maybe not. But your bookmakers like it because your bills are paid. Your bank account likes it because it's being fed regularly for the first time in a long time. And I like it because . . . because I like it."

"Join me for a drink?" Demmet asked, waving his glass slightly.

"How about taking a break? You're in surgery this afternoon, aren't you?"

"Yes," he said glumly. "But I can go in as drunk as I want to today. I don't have to kill anybody. Keeping people alive I can do drunk *or* sober. But killing people, for that only sober will do."

"Don't get maudlin on me. I don't have time today to hold your hand."

"No?"

"No. A very important person has checked into the Robler Clinic."

"Let's kill him right away. Before he has a chance to bitch about the meals."

"This is one we want to keep alive."

"What makes him different?"

"No one knows yet," Kathy Hahl said. "He's traveling under the name of Williams. He's brought his own doctor and he paid twenty-five thousand dollars cash in advance for the use of hospital facilities."

"Williams? I don't know any famous Williamses."

"Obviously, that's not his real name. But I'll find out who he really is. It could well be that he might like to donate some money to Robler in the event of his sudden demise."

"Well, until you decide to zap him, he's no concern of mine. And even then, he might not be."

"What does that mean?" Kathy Hahl demanded.

"I don't like this crap any more. There's just too many of them. And Mrs. Wilberforce was an ugly old ox, but she didn't have anything to do with anything. Not really."

"She was a threat. The way to handle threats is to eliminate them."

"That's the way to handle thirst, too. You're not going to have a drink with me?" Demmet asked.

"No," Kathy Hahl said. She smiled, but there was no humor in the movement of her lips. The smile was steely, micrometer precise, and totally without warmth.

"Well, somebody else will, I suppose," Demmet said angrily. He walked out of the office angrily.

Kathy Hahl watched the door close behind him, then looked down at the glass on her desk and at the gold ring.

Dr. Daniel Demmet might be getting cold feet. That would make him both dangerous and—if the experiment on Mrs. Wilberforce worked as well as it did on Anthony Stace—expendable.

She put the golden ring into her handbag until she had a chance to refill it.

CHAPTER TEN

Mrs. Wilberforce was found where Dr. Demmet had left her, in the bed of her motel room.

He had taken her in the early morning hours. It had been so long since she had had a man. It had been so long. She had abused men and browbeaten them, and when there were no real men around, she had used her son as a surrogate man, trying to break his spirit and will and body. But then when Demmet had just gone ahead and made love to her, without concern for her feelings, almost as if his mind were not there, she realized that she had wanted all the while for a man to rebel against her and to take her.

Demmet did and left her in the bed, thinking how pleasant the sex was, and how impossible it was that the nice Dr. Demmet could have been any part of a cover up involving Nathan David's death. He had told her how hard he had tried to save him, but how there was nothing he could do.

She thought about that just before closing her eyes and trying to sleep. But sleep would not come. First, there was a pain in the left temple and then a pain in the right temple, and then a continuous throbbing pain that made it feel as if there were something inside her head, pounding, trying to tear its way out.

She had gotten up and made her way to the bathroom of the small motel room, and from her personal kit had taken a small bottle of aspirins. She downed two of them. As she threw her head back to swallow the water from the small paper cup, her eyes caught sight of her reflection in the mirror of the medicine cabinet.

She looked at herself, then leaned forward to examine her face carefully. Sex was supposed to rejuvenate people, she had thought. Put on the glow of happiness. But there was no glow in her face. There were wrinkles at the corners of her eyes and heavy bags under her eyes. And there had been no wrinkles and no bags early in the day. The headache, she decided, was worse than she thought. It must really have been wreaking havoc with her system to do that to her face. She hoped that the headache was only a headache, not the first symptom of whatever terrible illness it was that Nathan David had caught. Pneumonia. That would be terrible. Though of course she would have that nice Dr. Demmet to nurse her back to health.

She went back to bed, trying not to think of her headache, but it was five in the morning before she finally fell asleep.

She slept past her usual wakeup time of 6:45. A maid came into the room at 9:30, saw her in bed and sneaked out again. When the maid came back at 12:30, she still saw no do-not-disturb sign on the door, went in and saw Mrs. Wilberforce still asleep in the bed. She became suspicious this time and called softly to try to awaken her. But there was no response from the bed.

The maid called the manager who had checked Mrs. Wilberforce in the day before.

"What is it?" the manager asked when he finally

made his way to the room. "I hope it's important."

"This woman won't wake up," the maid said. "I think she's sick."

The manager paused in the doorway. "Let's see," he said. "Oh yes, this is Mrs. Wilberforce. She checked in yesterday." He stood hesitantly in the open doorway of the room. "Mrs. Wilberforce," he called. "Mrs. Wilberforce." There was no movement under the covers.

"Mrs. Wilberforce," he called again, this time loudly.

"She won't answer," the maid said. "I think she's sick."

"Well, she'd better be sick or your ass is going to be in real trouble," hissed the manager, who had adopted this manner of speaking to the young Puerto Rican maid after the girl had committed the unpardonable sin of refusing to spend an afternoon with him in one of the motel's empty rooms and, even worse, threatened to tell his wife if he should persist in asking.

The manager swallowed once. Invading women's bedrooms was not the kind of thing managers did happily. "You keep your twiff right here," he whispered to the girl, making sure that he had a witness to his entry. He brushed past the girl brusquely and walked around the edge of the bed.

He began to call Mrs. Wilberforce's name to the form hidden under the covers. There was still no response. He gently grabbed a section of blanket that he thought concealed an arm. He shook slightly.

"Mrs. Wilberforce."

There was a faint groan from under the blanket. Carefully, the manager pulled the cover down from the face of the person under the blanket. He paused, looking at the face, then recoiled sharply.

"This isn't Mrs. Wilberforce," he said excitedly.

"It isn't?" said the girl, moving into the room.

"No. Come look," he said, waving the girl forward. She walked nearer, at first hesitantly, then boldly. She came around to the side of the manager and looked down at the face of the figure in the bed. Involuntarily, she let out a gasp.

The face that lay there was as ugly as sin, as old as time. The skin was dried and brown with the deep cracked-mud wrinkles of extreme age. The hair was gray and there were occasional long hairs jutting out from the cheeks, the chin—long white wiry hairs, the kind grown by witches.

"Mrs. Wilberforce is a much younger woman," the manager said. "I checked her in yesterday myself. This isn't her."

The head on the pillow moved slightly. Muscles in the eyelids seemed to flicker and then slowly, as if waiting for death to come and grant her reprieve, the rheumy eyes opened and looked blankly at the man and woman by the bed.

The lips moved slightly, but there was no sound. They moved again, the muscles at the corners of the mouth twitching spasmodically, and then the mouth opened and a tired scratch leaked out:

"I am Mrs. Wilberforce."

Chiun was watching television and Remo was lying on the couch practicing meditation when the telephone next to the green velvet sofa rang.

"This is Smith," said the voice, all lemons and bitternesses. "I have just learned that Mrs. Wilberforce . . . I believe you met her . . . has been taken to Robler Clinic."

"What's wrong with her?"

"I don't know. She was found sick in her motel

room outside the city about an hour ago. You understand the connection, of course?"

"First her son, then her. Why, I don't know."

"Try to find out."

"Anything new elsewhere? Anything come up with the IRS investigations?"

"Nothing that we know of. Whatever Wilberforce may have been working on was largely in his head. We'll probably never know. Keep in touch. By the way, this line is secure. We've had our own men check it."

Remo slowly returned the receiver to the telephone, then hopped off the couch. He looked at Chiun's back, who appeared to be in a trance, fixated by the images on the television screen. No need to bother him, particularly since there was no chance of bothering him. Chiun would not move from the set until his shows were over. The room could be bombed, flooded or set afire. When the smoke had cleared, the water subsided and the debris settled, Chiun would still be there in full lotus watching Dr. Lance Ravenel solving the problems of the world with wisdom and kindness.

Remo wore a tan tee-shirt, brown double-knit slacks and gumsoled glove-leather slipons that were handmade in Italy.

"Well, I'm going now, Chiun," he said loudly.

There was no answer.

"I may never return. This is my most dangerous mission," Remo said.

Silence.

"Yet it is a far far better thing I do than I have ever done," Remo said.

"Almost anything is," Chiun spat back, and then was silent again, leaving only the television's voice in the room.

"Chiun, you're a shit," Remo yelled.

But there was no answer again, and Remo slipped on the dark glasses, which he did not really like to wear, and the wearing of which infuriated Chiun.

Remo had bought them while wandering the streets of San Francisco late one afternoon with Chiun. San Francisco was one of their favorite cities, because its cosmopolitan polyglot nature found nothing unusual about an eighty-year-old Oriental in ceremonial robes walking along the street with a hard-faced lean-looking American, and just as long as Remo kept Chiun away from Chinatown, they had never been hassled in San Francisco.

This day, they wandered into Union Square and Chiun insisted upon going into a large department store there.

Remo had gone to look at golf clubs. When he came back, he found Chiun in a corner of the store's ground floor, watching an optometrist fit a woman with eyeglasses.

Chiun was clucking loudly. The eye doctor and the woman kept turning to glare at him, and Chiun glared back.

"What are you doing, Little Father?" Remo had asked.

"Watching this man ruin that woman's eyes."

"Shhhh," said Remo. "Somebody will hear you."

"Good," Chiun said. "Think how many eyes I can save if all will but listen."

"Chiun. Some people need glasses."

"Wrong. No one needs the glasses for seeing."

"Sure they do. You've seen those funny little eye charts that all start with E. Some people can't read the letters."

"Ahah, but they do not spell words," said Chiun triumphantly. "Who would want to read the letters?"

111

"That's not the point. Some people just can't even see what the letters are."

"That is because their eye muscles do not work correctly. The muscles are untrained. Yet, instead of training the muscles to work properly, what do people do? They go to a so-called doctor who puts these pieces of glass in front of their eyes. This makes sure that the person will never have a chance to train the eye muscles to work correctly. It is a terrible thing this man is doing."

"Some people can't control their eye muscles," Remo said in mild protest.

"That is true," Chiun agreed. "Most of them are Americans. This country is a cesspool of laziness. We have been many places, but only in this place do you find almost everyone wearing eyeglasses. Do you need any further proof of laziness?"

"That's not true, Chiun. One of the reasons many people in this country have eye trouble is from watching television."

Chiun's mouth dropped open in amazement. "You lie," he said.

"No, it's true. Too much television hurts the eyes."

"Oh," moaned Chiun. "Oh, the infamy. Do you tell me that those beautiful dramas could harm my eyes?"

"Well, maybe not yours. But most people's."

"Oh, the infamy. To say such a thing, and only to hurt my feelings." He looked at Remo questioningly.

Remo shook his head. "Truth, Little Father."

Chiun was silent momentarily, considering the terribleness of it all, then smiled craftily and raised a long-nailed index finger into the air. "Ahhh," he said, "even suppose what you say is true. Think of how much good these beautiful dramas do for the soul and the heart."

Remo sighed. "That's true enough, Little Father.

112

They're beautiful. They enrich everyone's life, blind or sighted. I'd rather have the whole country go blind than to have the wonderfulness of those shows reduced by even so much as one minute."

"There is hope for you yet, Remo," said Chiun. "But not for him," he said, pointing to the eye doctor. "He should tell these people to exercise their eye muscles, not to wrap them up in a glass bandage that prevents them from ever using their eyes correctly."

"What is all this noise?" came a woman's voice. It came from a young blonde with a Scandinavian accent, who had come out of the back room of the optical department.

To quiet her down, Remo had bought a pair of almost black sunglasses, even though he did not like wearing them. Chiun was, of course, right. Left alone, the trained eye muscle was more than able to screen out light, to let in light, to focus, to see. Sunglasses were just another crutch for a muscular cripple.

As he tried on different frames, Chiun had demanded of the woman that she try to find him a pair of spectacles that did not use glass but had wooden lenses. "Since he insists upon ruining his vision, we should at least protect him from flying glass."

Remo had settled for the darkest pair of lenses he could find. He stuck the glasses in his pocket and had not worn them until entering the Robler Clinic, when they became part of his billionaire's disguise.

Remo heard the organ music come up and over signifying a commercial and Chiun turned to see Remo in his dark glasses.

"That is very good," said Chiun. "You come to this hospital looking for something and the first thing you do is cover over your eyes so you cannot see. A truly American approach to a problem." He turned back to the television, consigning Remo to a lower rung on the ladder of his interest than a horse-faced lady plumber selling soap.

Remo thumbed his nose at Chiun's back and stepped out into the hall.

The walls and floors were a creamy-tan marble and looked cold, but Remo touched a wall and found it warm. The latest innovation in heating. Warmed walls. Obviously, Robler Clinic did not worry about where its next buck was coming from

Three doors down from his room, he saw a closet and slipped inside. On a top shelf he found what he wanted; when he exited a few moments later, he was wearing a full-length white medical gown.

With his sunglasses and gown, he looked like a hungover playboy which, Remo decided, characterized most of the doctors he had ever known.

He went down to the fourth floor by the stairs and rudely interrupted a nurse talking on a telephone at a desk. "Where is the emergency room?"

"First floor, doctor," she answered. "That elevator over there."

"Your collar's getting a little frayed, nurse," said Remo. "Better watch that."

"Yes sir, doctor," she said, and, puzzled, watched as he walked away. She wondered who he was.

Remo decided to walk to the emergency room and was astonished as he made his way through the hospital corridors to the action center of the hospital. No one stopped him; no one questioned who he was. He could have accepted that if it were obvious that people thought he was a doctor and asked him to do doctorly things. But no one did. He stuck his head into different examining rooms, looking for Mrs. Wilberforce, but no one asked his advice or help.

He had physical acceptance in that his presence was tolerated, but he did not have professional acceptance, as no one had asked him for help. He did not know if this were good or bad, but he decided it was insulting and caused by his lack of a stethoscope. As he passed a doctor in the hall, he filched the stethoscope from around the man's neck, snaking it off his collar with a finger. The doctor kept walking ahead, unmindful of his loss, and Remo put the stethoscope around his own neck.

The stethoscope worked wonders. Before he had gone fifty feet more, Remo was asked for advice on three separate cases

He stuck his head in one room, stethoscope dangling from his ears, and was asked his opinion about a patient suffering a broken leg. He prescribed aspirin and plenty of bed rest. He called another patient a faker, using up hospital space that was needed by really sick people. In the third room, he had his first chance to use the stethoscope. He was amazed that one could really hear things through it.

A fat woman lay on an examining table, being examined by a young man in white gown, obviously an intern. He looked up hopefully as Remo came in.

Remo placed the stethoscope on the woman's stomach and broke out laughing. "Listen to that rumbling," he said. "Wow, what a racket. It sounds like pea soup cooking."

"What do you think, doctor?" asked the intern.

"I'd say two tablespoons of Pepto Bismol every three hours ought to do the trick. And you, lady, you better knock off the beer."

The intern moved closer to Remo and whispered in his ear: "But it's the headaches she's complaining of."

Remo nodded officiously. "Right," he said. "That comes from the beer. It's the yeast in the beer. It blows up inside the body and the gas causes pressure

115

in the skull cavity. I remember hearing Brother Theodore explain that at the last medical lecture I went to. Watch that yeast. And you, lady, knock off the beer."

"Well, I never . . ." the woman said to Remo's back.

He paused at the door, turned, smiled and said, "Don't worry about the bill either. Just send it to me."

Then he was out in the hallway, moving along, hoping for someone else to try his stethoscope on.

At the end of the corridor were a heavy pair of metal swinging doors with large wired glass panels in them. Remo glanced through the panels then pushed open a door. He was, he realized, in the emergency room complex.

There were four rooms; all but one were empty. In that one, he found Mrs. Wilberforce. Going in the door, he found a face mask in the pocket of his gown and put it on.

There was a figure on the emergency table, partially covered by sparkling white sheets, and around her hovered a team of men and women, doctors and nurses, all busy. Two nurses massaged the patient's legs and feet. A doctor and nurse were leaning on the chest area, rhythmically, in a kind of team artificial-respiration effort.

Remo's eyes were drawn to another doctor who was standing alongside the patient drawing a fluid into a syringe, possibly for injection into the heart, which would make it adrenalin.

That doctor did not look happy, Remo thought. He watched the man's hands holding the syringe and the small adrenalin ampule, saw them shake, and realized what was wrong—the doctor had been drinking.

Remo moved into the room, whistling softly, the whistle turning into a hiss of air through his mask.

116

A few heads turned toward him.

"Hi, folks," he said. "Just keep doing what you're doing. If I spot anything wrong, I'll let you know."

He lifted his stethoscope in reassurance. Faces turned back toward the patient.

Casually, Remo walked up to the side of the patient. It was a woman, but an aged woman, as Remo could see in glimpses of her face when a young nurse sporadically removed the oxygen mask from her nose and mouth. Remo thought back to the visit to Mrs. Wilberforce in Scranton, the big, buxom battleaxe he had slapped on the rump. Then he looked down on the shriveled old woman, lying in the bed.

Dammit, he thought. Where is Mrs. Wilberforce?

He turned to go, but as he did, his eyes caught sight of a magic-markered name tag on the head of the bed. "Wilberforce," it read.

He looked again at the face of the woman. How could it be? But the eyes . . . the hooked nose . . . it might be . . . it could be. He looked again, hard. It was. But how? A few days ago, she had looked like a member of the Praetorian Guard, but now she was small and weak, frail and *old*.

How could it be?

He looked again at the doctor who, still shakily, had finished filling the syringe. Behind the patient, an electrocardiogram screen was jumping erratically. The artificial respiration continued; the extremity massage went on.

Another person came into the room. Like the doctor with the syringe, she did not wear a hospital robe. She was wearing a tight yellow sweater and a short white skirt that showed off long, full legs.

She entered the room imperiously, as if she owned the hospital. A nurse caught sight of the movement at the door and looked up as if to reprimand the

117

visitor, but when she saw who it was, she turned back to her massage of the right leg.

The reddish-haired beauty walked up and stood alongside the man with the syringe.

"How is it going, Dr. Demmet?" she said.

"Serious case, Ms. Hahl," he answered. His voice was wavering, cracky.

"Oh?"

"General breakdown of body functions. Advanced senility."

"Can you save her?"

"I don't know," the doctor said.

"Try to," the woman said. Her eyes met the doctor's. "Try to," she said again. It was almost like a challenge, Remo thought.

"I'm going to," the doctor said.

"You do that. You do that."

The doctor leaned forward, inserted the syringe between the woman's ribs and injected the jolt of adrenalin directly into her heart.

The woman in the yellow sweater watched detachedly for a moment, then looked around the room. Her eyes stopped on Remo, standing behind the crowd of doctors and nurses. He realized how out of place he must look with his black sunglasses.

The woman came to his side.

"Who might you be?" she asked.

Remo decided he would be eccentric.

"Williams my name, sickness my game."

"Williams? Are you *the* Mr. Williams?"

Remo nodded. He could see the woman was impressed. Her fine, intelligent eyes lit up as if illuminated from within.

"But why are you here?" she asked.

"I like hospitals. I always wanted to be a doctor. I play golf every Wednesday. I own my own stethoscope. I wanted to be here. I wouldn't have missed it."

Kathy Hahl nodded. "I'm Kathy Hahl, the assistant administrator. I've been meaning to check with you to see if there was anything you needed."

Remo shook his head. "Nope. Having a great time right here, watching these fine people work on that poor old lady. Funny thing. I hear she's not as old as she looks."

"So I'm told," Kathy Hahl said.

"Unusual case," Remo said.

Kathy Hahl nodded.

"Kind of instant aging," Remo said. "Never heard of anything like that before."

"I understand it happens sometimes. A shock to the nervous system can do it. I understand this woman recently lost a son she was very close to."

Remo did not answer. He was watching the doctor at the side of the bed. What was his name . . . Dr. Demmet? He was pounding on the woman's chest with a fist. The electrocardiogram was now smoothly beeping along, rolling hills, gentle valleys. Demmet pounded hard. "Live, Goddamnit, live," he cried.

"Ummmm," Remo said. "Yes, a shock. Her son, Nathan. They were very close." As he watched the doctor, he did not see the glint in Kathy Hahl's eyes as he mentioned the name "Nathan." No one had said anything about a Nathan. She suddenly realized that Mr. Williams was not just an eccentric billionaire; he was something more. And dangerous.

Demmet clenched his fists and shook them in front of his own face in frustration. "All right," he said, his voice heavy and sullen. "You can stop now. She's gone."

He looked up to where Remo and Kathy Hahl stood.

"I couldn't save her," he said to Kathy Hahl across Mrs. Wilberforce's dead body.

"That's a terrible shame, Dr. Demmet," Kathy Hahl said, and Remo thought he detected sarcasm. "Beyond the reach of your medical skill, no doubt."

Demmet looked at her, then down at the patient, and as Remo watched, the anger at her death seemed to drain from his face, and was replaced by something resembling relief. He paused a moment, then turned and walked out of the emergency room. Now that was strange, Remo thought. Dr. Demmet might bear some watching.

"He seems to be taking it very hard," Remo said conversationally to Kathy Hahl.

"Yes," she said. "Some doctors get personally involved. It makes their lives difficult." She paused, then said brightly, "And you, Mr. Williams, has everything been all right?"

"Fine," Remo said.

"Medical service all right?"

"I don't know. I've brought my own physician. He won't let anybody else touch me."

"Plan to be here long?" she asked.

What'd she say she was? Assistant administrator? That might do. She might be just the person to put out the rumor Remo wanted put out around the hospital.

He leaned over to her conspiratorially. "Not too long. Just until some Internal Revenue wiseguys get off my back."

"Oh, I see. Tax problems."

"The curse of the billionaire class," Remo said.

"Well, let's hope they resolve themselves."

"Yes, let's hope."

"I live in the hospital, Mr. Williams. The switchboard can always reach me. If you want anything . . .

anything at all, or if I can help, don't hesitate to call me at any hour. Day or night." She looked at Remo with a gaze that was all electric.

By the time he got back to his room, Remo felt pretty good. In the hospital only a few hours and already he had a suspect in that Dr. Demmet. And he had already put out the word that he had tax problems and might be appreciative of some help in getting rid of them. That might promote an offer. All in all, a good day's work. All head and no muscle. No more Scrantons. He would intellect his way through this case. Yes, he would. And when he was done and he had tied up the solution neatly, with no blood and no killing, why Smith would be delighted and even Chiun would have to admit that Remo could figure out a thing or two.

Yes, indeed.

In Remo's view, a plan planned was as good as an act acted. He already tasted the glow of victory. He paused outside his hospital suite, then pushed open the door and jumped into the room, his white robe swirling about him, his stethoscope flopping against his chest.

"Da daaaaaa," he trumpeted.

"What is this *da daaaaa?*" asked Chiun who was now seated at the window, looking out over the hideousness which was downtown Baltimore a few miles away.

"That's called a triumphant entry," said Remo. "I am Dr. Lance Ravenel come to save the world from the agony of psoriasis."

"Silence your face," said Chiun. "Dr. Ravenel is no fit subject for your retarded sense of levity."

"Ummmm," said Remo, feeling as if the air of joy had been squooshed out of him. "Is that so?"

"Yes, that is so. Dr. Ravenel is a noble member of a noble profession. The profession of healing. You see how he makes people well again in the beautiful stories."

"Those are only stories."

"There is more truth in those stories than in your so-called facts," Chiun said.

"Pfooey."

"Do you tell me there is no truth in how Dr. Ravenel heals the ill?"

"Remember in San Francisco? You told me illness is a sign of lack of discipline on the part of the patient? You've changed your mind?"

"No. That is what causes illness. But if doctors cannot get people to think right and end their illness, then they must do it some other way. It is a gift they have. You should not denigrate. Least of all, you, who have no gifts at all."

"Since when did you become a spokesman for the AMA?"

"I do not know what it is, this AMA, but if it involves speaking only the truth, then I am for it."

Remo only grunted, thoroughly down now after having been so up. Victory no longer seemed as assured as it had when he jumped through the door. There was work yet to be done.

And he had something else to think about. The aging of Mrs. Wilberforce had been nagging at his brain, and he realized now what it reminded him of. Anthony Stace in Scranton. Remo had been looking for a vigorous middle-aged man and instead had found a parchment-brittle old specter who seemed to welcome death in preference to being old.

Had it happened to him, too? That sudden aging? And what was it he had told Remo? "Stay away from

122

hospitals." *Had* it happened to him too? Kathy Hahl had said shock could produce that kind of effect, but Remo had never heard of shock this severe.

"Chiun, how does a man grow old?"

"By donating the best years of his life to an ungrateful whelp who does not even acknowledge the finest of gifts." Chiun was still angry.

"Chiun, for a minute, forget Barbra Streisand. I just saw a woman die. Three days ago, she was a big, strong, loud hulk who could've busted a bear's back."

"It sounds like no great loss," Chiun said.

"No. But just now, she looked a hundred years old. She was thin and wrinkled. Dammit, Chiun, she was *old*. And a week ago, I ran into a man who was the same way. Overnight, he had aged."

"And you do not understand it?"

"No," Remo said.

"There are many things in the world we do not understand. How does an American meat-eater learn the secrets of Sinanju? What makes him able to climb a wall, to break a bond, to withstand a potion?"

Remo waited for Chiun to answer his own questions as he usually did, but there was no answer. Remo said, "I changed, Chiun. That's how I was able to do these things."

"And you changed because you willed yourself to change."

"Are you saying these people got old because they willed themselves to?"

"No," Chiun said. "I say they grew old because they did not will themselves to stay young. Perhaps one of your country's special medicines made them old. But it could not have happened unless they allowed it. No one changes unless he allows himself

123

to change. They grow old only who have been waiting to grow old."

"Thank you for no answer at all."

"Call upon me anytime," Chiun said, and returned his gaze to the window.

CHAPTER ELEVEN

"His name is Doctor Demmet. No, I don't know the first name. Just Demmet."

"A minute," Smith said. "Let me run that through the computer."

Remo heard the telephone being placed down, then he heard Smith working at the small computer console in his office. Thirty seconds later, the phone was picked up.

"If there is anything, we should have it in a minute or so," Smith said. "What about this Demmet? Why him?"

"I don't really know," Remo said. "It was just the look on his face in the emergency room." Remo thought back, saw again Demmet's strained thin-lipped face, his obvious mixed emotions when Mrs. Wilberforce began to sink. His frenzied effort to save her, to keep her alive, but then the look of relief on his face when there was nothing else he could do for her. "It was just the way he looked," Remo said again.

"Not much in the way of concrete information," Smith said drily. "Hardly twenty-five-thousand dollars worth."

"Well, actually," Remo said testily, "I was thinking

of distributing a questionnaire to the staff here. Which one of you is a killer? If not you, list five suspects in descending order of probability. Then when I get them all together, I was going to ship them to you and you could run them through that idiot computer, which would probably decide that the guilty party was me. Dammit, of course I don't have anything concrete yet. I just got here."

"Wait," Smith interrupted. "The printout's coming."

He paused for a full minute, then began to read:

"Demmet, Daniel, M.D. Born in Elkton, Maryland."

"Skip the who's who. Get on with it, please," Remo said.

Smith paused a moment, then said, "Demmet was one of the consulting physicians when Nathan Wilberforce died. He was the anesthesiologist when Boulder, the IRS man, died."

"Is that concrete enough for you?" Remo gloated.

"It is highly suggestive," Smith said.

"Suggestive, my left nostril. It's solid."

"Suggestive. I'd keep a weather eye on Demmet if I were you."

"Thank you," Remo said testily. "And if you were me, what would you do if you saw a woman age forty years in a couple of days?"

"What is that supposed to mean?" Remo realized that suddenly Smith was fully attentive.

He told the director about Anthony Stace, and then about Mrs. Wilberforce. There was silence on the phone when he finished.

"Not so quick with your suggestions now, are you?" Remo said. "You sometimes seem to have the idea it's easy out here in the field. I don't think you have any real concept of the kind of work I do."

"Mediocre work, generally," Smith said. "On the

aging business, I have no explanation. I'll try to get autopsy reports on the two bodies."

"You do that. You do that. And in the meantime, I'll stay here doing the hard, difficult work that solves problems like this."

"I'm touched," Smith said. "I hadn't realized how hard you work."

"That's the trouble," Remo said. "No one realizes how hard I work."

"I'll keep it in mind." Smith hung up.

Remo put the phone carefully back, restraining his impulse to break it into little plastic chips, only because the bill for the phone would go to Smith and he didn't want to have to put up with that again. He looked around the large sitting room, illuminated now only by the conical splash of light from the high-intensity lamp on the wall over his head.

Chiun slept on a thin mat in a corner of the room. Remo watched him, then went into the bedroom and lay on the bed. Slowly, he began to breathe deeply, down into the pit of his stomach, to try to rid himself of his tension and annoyance. Breathe. Deep. Down into the groin. Hold it. Release. Two counts for inhale. Two counts for hold. Two counts for slow exhale. He did it again and again. And again.

The breathing exercise blotted out his surroundings. His perceptions eased. His level of consciousness lowered. Tension began to drain from his body and mind. Pure silence. Pure rest.

"Hnnnnnkkkkk." The noise was like an unoiled buzz saw ripping wet green wood. It went through Remo's ears like an icepick. What the hell was that?

"Hnnnnnnkkkkk" came the sound again, even louder this time.

It was Chiun. Snoring.

"Knock that off, Chiun," Remo yelled at the open door.

"Hnnnnnnkkkkkk."

"Oh, for Christ's sake," Remo growled. He got up out of the bed and slammed the door.

Before he returned to his bed, it came again.

"Hnnnnnnkkkkkk."

Remo went out into the sitting room and looked over at the sleeping Chiun.

What he would have liked to do would have been to go over to Chiun and put his toe into Chiun's side and get him to stop the snoring. What he would not have liked would have been the broken leg, or worse, that would be sure to follow.

"How's a guy supposed to sleep around here?" he asked aloud.

"Hnnnnnnkkkkkk."

Remo slipped on his gumsoled shoes and walked out into the now darkened hospital hallway. His annoyance bubbled in him and momentarily he considered introducing the entire hospital staff to Remo's unique of way of observing the Feast of the Pig. No. Smith would go nuts over another Scranton.

Instead he walked the corridors, at first hearing his gumsoled shoes squish against the highly polished marble floor, then trying to forget his mind in his body, and practicing walking silently, soundlessly.

He found a dark corridor around the corner from his room, and began to practice the Ninja side crawl. He stood with his back to the wall, then began to move down the hallway, left foot crossing over right, right left lifting and extending full, then left over again. Back and forth, he did it, faster and faster, until he was moving with the speed of a sprinter. Four times down the corridor, four times back. It did no good, and on his last return trip, he heard his gumsole squeak once on the final move, and the sloppiness only increased his annoyance.

He ran straight up along the corridor, through a fire door, down to the next floor, along the corridor, down another flight of steps to the next floor, along another corridor, practicing moving silently, and he finally pushed open a fire door, to find himself in the hallway next to the clinic's main lobby. He still was not tired, he was not breathing hard, and he wasn't at peace with himself.

He went back up the stairs to the fifth floor, and moved away from his room, down a long corridor to the back section of the new wing where there were more patient's rooms. He stood listening to the breathing of the patients. A nurse's station should be down the hall and he turned his hearing in that direction. He could hear a ball point pen skidding through its greasy ink across a piece of paper. The nurse was there writing. But maybe it wasn't the nurse. He listened harder. He could hear the faint rustling crackle of a hard fabric, moving in unison with the pen. It was probably a nurse's nylon uniform. Good enough, he thought.

He trained his attention on the door of the third room down the hall. It was slightly ajar.

Remo tried to blot out all other sounds on the floor. He listened intently. Yes. Two people were in that room. Both men. No, wait. One was a woman. The man's breath was shallow and nasal. The woman's breath deeper and slower.

No, Remo, you're wrong. What would a woman be doing in a hospital room with a man?

He listened again. No. It was a man and a woman. Even if it shouldn't be.

That would be all he needed tonight to make the evening complete, a failure on his listening exercises.

He moved along the near wall until he was opposite the slightly opened door. He still could not see the nurse—if it was a nurse—at her desk.

He moved across the marble floor through the swinging door into the dark room. There were two beds there. A man in one, a woman in another.

Okay. The hearing had been right. He felt pretty good. Still he wondered what a man and woman were doing in the same room. What was this—a coed hospital? Was nothing sacred anymore?

Feeling relieved and rested, he walked out into the hallway. He looked down the hall and saw the nurse at her station, writing patients' reports. She chose that moment to look up and see him. Her face widened with surprise. Her hand instinctively reached for the telephone.

Remo walked toward her, smiling.

"Hi," he said.

"Who are you?" she said, her hand still on the telephone.

"Well, actually, I'm an undercover investigator for the state anti-vice and morals commission and I'm wondering what that man and woman are doing together in Room 561."

"That's Mr. Downheimer. His wife is staying with him while he recovers from surgery. But who said you could come up here?"

"Nothing stops me in the search for immorality," Remo said. "It must be rooted out wherever it is, if we're going to preserve the moral fiber of the republic. This is a republic, you know, and not a democracy."

"But . . ."

"A lot of people think it's a democracy, but it's not really. Ask Chiun. He thinks it's an empire, but actually that's wrong too, you know. A republic. That's all, a republic."

"I think I'm going to call an attendant," she said, lifting the receiver.

"I never met an attendant who knew the difference between a democracy and a republic," Remo said. "But if you think he can take part in our conversation, why go ahead and call him. Actually, though, it was getting late and I was going to leave."

"The attendant will show you out," she said.

"Out? I'm not going out. I'm just going back to my room."

"Where's your room?" The nurse was blonde and pert, and wore a name tag of Nancy. Remo thought for a moment to invite her to his room. But no, Chiun would get upset. Besides she looked like a good nurse and that meant she wouldn't leave her station.

"I'm in Room 515," Remo said. "Over that way." He jerked a thumb over his shoulder. "Mr. Williams."

"The Mr. Williams?"

"I don't know if I'm the Mr. Williams. I'm just plain old Mr. Williams. Just another average, fun-loving, tax-dodging billionaire hermit."

The nurse was flustered. "Oh. Oh." She took her hand away from the telephone. "I had heard you were on this floor, but I never thought I'd see you."

"Do me a favor, Nancy, and don't tell anyone else I'm here. I don't want reporters around. Okay?"

"Sure."

"Good. You working again tomorrow night?"

The nurse nodded.

"Fine. Maybe I'll sneak out to see you again and we can talk some more."

"That would be nice."

Remo turned to his right from the desk, toward

a set of double doors. The doors had a plastic red and white sign mounted that read:

NO TRESPASSING. KEEP OUT. VISITORS NOT PERMITTED.

"You can't go through that way, Mr. Williams," the nurse called.

"Oh? What's in here?"

"The hospital's research laboratories. No one's permitted in there. You'll have to take the long way around."

"Okay," Remo said. "See you tomorrow." He smiled at her and began to run quietly down the hall.

By the time he got back to his suite, he felt better. Nurse Nancy had been pleasant, he had gotten rid of his anger and tension, and he hadn't even had to kill anyone.

He lay down in bed, smiling slightly to himself, feeling at peace with the world, and before he dozed off the last thing he heard was:

"Hnnnnnnkkkk."

"Damned Chinaman," he hissed to himself and fell asleep, but not before pondering what might be behind those closed doors of the research laboratories.

CHAPTER TWELVE

"I did not sleep all night." Chiun had donned a long green robe and stood looking out the window of the sitting room.

"You didn't?" said Remo.

"No. I kept waking up, hearing this awful sound. But when I awoke, I saw nothing. I heard nothing. It was very strange. Did you not hear it?"

"Was it a long, terrible sound, like a crazy goose? Sort of a 'hnnnnkkkkkkk'?"

"Yes. That was it."

"No. I didn't hear it. We will watch for it together tonight."

Chiun searched his face for something less than honesty, but saw nothing there except blandness.

"You are a good son at times."

"Thank you, Little Father."

"Even if you do not give me the only Christmas present I seek, after I made you that beautiful tree."

Remo looked away with a sigh. Someday, he might have to present Barbra Streisand to Chiun.

He showered and later asked Chiun, "What will you do today, Little Father?"

"I thought I would watch these marvelous doctors as they heal the sick and save the dying. Just like

Dr. Ravenel on the beautiful dramas. Am I allowed to do that?"

"Of course," said Remo. "You're that noted Korean physician, Dr. Park, aren't you?"

"And you?"

"Today, I'm going to look behind some closed doors," Remo said.

He wore his white doctor's gown, his stolen stethoscope and his black sunglasses as he strolled around the corridors to the research labs.

Remo paused in the corridor facing the doors, waiting to see if there was any pattern of movement in or out. His presence was ignored by nurses and doctors on the floor. He stuck his head into Room 561 where Mr. and Mrs. Downheimer were staying. They were sitting on the edges of their beds, the bedside cabinet between them, and playing Kalah, an ancient African game played with stones. Both looked up as Remo paused in the doorway.

"Good morning," he said.

"Good morning," Mrs. Downheimer answered.

"Enjoying your stay?" Remo asked.

"Yes, thank you."

"I looked in on you last night. You slept very soundly." Remo glanced over his shoulder along the corridor. Still no one at the door.

"Yes. I really feel rested," Mr. Downheimer said.

"Keep up the good work. Who's winning?"

"I am," Downheimer said.

"I am," Mrs. Downheimer said.

Remo heard feet moving toward the end of the corridor. "Well, take care yourselves now," he said, and backed out into the hall.

A big shouldered man in medical whites, with shoulder-length black greasy hair, was coming through

134

the double iron doors. They opened with a heavy squeak.

The man pushed the door shut behind him, then tested the handle to make sure it was locked. Satisfied, he walked down the corridor past Remo toward the elevator. As he passed Remo, he nodded. Remo nodded back. He was not sure whether the man was a doctor or not. He decided not because the man was not wearing a stethoscope, just as the man had decided Remo was a doctor because he was wearing one.

Remo stood in the doorway, watching the man's back until he turned the corner toward the bank of elevators. Remo waved to the Downheimers again, walked toward the end of the corridor and the heavy iron doors. Casually, he passed the nurse's station, nodding to the nurse on duty. She said politely, "Good morning, doctor," then watched as he made for the doors.

He fumbled in the pocket of his medical gown, clicking his fingernails together to simulate the sound of keys clacking on a ring. He put his body between the nurse and the doorknob, mimed inserting a key into the lock, then with his left hand, crushed the door handle, pressing it past the locking pin until the handle gave way and the door bolt slid free.

He returned his imaginary keys to his pocket, turned and smiled at the nurse and went in through the right hand door, pulling it shut tightly behind him.

He was in a large room, filled with sound. Off to the left were a string of small offices, and to the right was a large laboratory that reminded Remo of chemistry labs he had seen back in Weequahic High School in Newark.

Except for the sound.

The room was filled with cages. The cages were filled with lab animals—rats, cats, dogs, a few monkeys. Their combined noises were a roaring din, and Remo realized the heavy reinforcement of the doors had screened the ruckus from the outside halls.

In the back of the lab room were long tables. Other tables were interspersed between the cages. Racks of test tubes and instruments were on the tables. Along the side walls, partially obscuring the view from the windows, were tall white cabinets. One was half open and in it Remo could see supplies of chemicals and drugs in little bottles and flasks.

Remo moved into the room and the animals hushed. He could feel their eyes on him, watching him move.

Now what? He realized what a waste of time the whole idea had been. So the hospital had a private research lab. What in the hell did that have to do with anything, except research?

For a moment, he considered leaving, then shrugged and moved in among the cages.

The first cage contained a black alley cat. On the front of the cage was a neatly labeled sign that read: "Clyde. Born 11/14/72." The cat watched Remo insolently as he read the white tag. The cat licked its lips. Remo stuck a finger into the cage to tickle the cat's neck. The cat retreated to the far side of the cage, cringing.

Not much of a cat, Remo decided, and moved to the next cage.

It held another cat, also black, but this one's facial whiskers were grayed and the animal was emaciated. It lay quietly in a corner of the cage and as Remo stepped in front of the wire mesh, it rose to its feet with great effort and obvious discomfort and stood in the center of the cage. The cat yawned, so Remo could see many of its teeth were missing—its gums were old, wrinkled and dark.

It looked like the grandfather of all cats. No: grandmother. Remo looked at the tag on the cage:

"Naomi. Born 11/14/72."

"Naomi," Remo said. "Nice Naomi." He stuck a finger into the cage and that cat looked at it in disdain, as if it were something the dog had dragged in. "Here, nice Naomi," Remo said softly.

The cat refused to move, refused to acknowledge his finger.

Remo shrugged. "To hell with you, cat," he said.

He began to walk away, toward the front door, when he paused. Something was wrong. What was it?

He turned back to the two cages. Clyde and Naomi. Mother and son? Grandmother and son? They looked it. Clyde was young and frisky; the other cat aged and tired. Poor old Naomi.

Old?

Remo went back and looked at the tag on the cage. Naomi. Born 11/14/72.

He looked at the other cage.

Clyde. Born 11/14/72.

The two cats were the same age. But how could that be? Clyde was young, healthy looking; the other cat old and tired. Was Remo finally onto something?

Remo walked along the other rows of cages. He saw that they were divided into pairs. In one side of the pair was a young animal; next to it an ancient specimen. But the tags all listed each animal in the pair as born on the same day. Someone, something, somehow had aged one of the animals.

The thing he had seen with Mrs. Wilberforce. Before that with Anthony Stace in Scranton.

Every animal pair in the lab was the same. One old,

one young, but the tags on the cage listing their ages as exactly the same. Packaged senility.

Remo was at the table in the back getting ready to look into the files when a voice came.

"Hey. What are you doing there?"

Remo turned. The burly man with the shoulder-length black hair stood inside the double doors. He moved forward quickly toward Remo.

"I said, what are you doing there?"

"I heard you. I'm not deaf."

"What are you doing?"

"It's all right," Remo said. "Doctor Demmet said it would be okay for me to look around."

"Well, he ain't got no right to give nobody permission to wander around in here. Who are you anyway?"

Another man came out of the office. He also wore the two-piece white medical uniform. He was young and blond and even bigger than the first man. He looked at Remo, then at the dark man inside the door.

"Who the hell is this guy, Freddy?" he asked.

"Damned if I know. You were supposed to be watching the place." To Remo, he said, "I asked you, who are you?"

"My name's Williams," Remo said.

"You a doctor?"

"No, actually, I'm a patient. But I heard so much about your wonderful experiments here with aging that I thought I'd like to see for myself. And Doctor Demmet said it would be all right."

"It's not all right. Not all right for nobody but us," Freddy, the dark-haired man, said. "Al," he added. "Call the boss, explain about this guy."

"That won't be necessary," Remo said. "I'm leaving." He moved away from the desk toward the bank of cages.

The black-haired man stepped forward to meet him.

"You're going to wait," he said coldly.

"If you insist," Remo said. The blond man went to one of the offices in the back. Remo looked to his side at the cages of Clyde and Naomi. With two flicks of his right hand, he opened both cage doors.

"Hey. What are you doing?" Freddy asked.

"Opening the cages."

He walked back along the aisles, opening cage doors. Freddy lunged for the cages of Clyde and Naomi, but before he could close them Clyde had hopped out onto the floor. "Stop that, you bastard," he yelled at Remo. Remo, whistling, continued along the aisles, flicking open cage doors. Freddy closed them as fast as he could, bellowing all the while. The noise brought the blond man out of his office.

He moved toward Remo, but before he could reach him, the floor of the laboratory was aclutter with animals. Two chimps were out, hopping up and down off cages, screeching at the top of their register. The young-looking chimp took a leap and landed on one of the lab tables where he began knocking over vials and test tubes.

"Catch that frigging monkey," Freddy yelled to Al, who brushed by Remo, ignoring him and chasing after the chimp.

Remo, still whistling, sauntered casually toward the front door of the lab. He let himself out, then as an afterthought, reached up to the overhead door stop and locked it open.

As he passed the nurse's desk, he leaned over her and said, "They'll be busy in there for a while. I wouldn't disturb them if I were you."

Just before he turned the corridor, leading to his room, Remo glanced back. A chimpanzee was running through the open door, with Freddy and Al racing along behind him.

"Happy Feast of the Pig," Remo called.

Behind him, he could hear the shrill chatter of the chimp and the heavy thudding of Freddy and Al's feet as they tried to corner him.

Hell of a way to run a hospital, with monkeys running around loose, he thought. Wait until Chiun heard about that.

But Chiun was not in his room. He was making his rounds.

"I am Doctor Park. What seems to be wrong here?"

The doctor at the bedside looked away from the patient, and at the tiny wizened Oriental in the green robe.

"Doctor who?" he asked.

"Doctor Park. I am here for consultation. Oh, I understand. You do not wish to talk in front of the patient. Correct technique. Step over here and tell me what is wrong."

Chiun stepped back. The tall, dark-haired doctor looked at him quizzically for a moment, then with an imperceptible shrug of the shoulders, stepped over to Chiun's side.

"The patient," he said softly, "is a middle-aged male. He has a stomach blockage of undetermined nature. Surgery is indicated."

"You are sure he is not faking?"

"Faking?"

"Yes. Most of the people here I believe are faking."

"Why?" the doctor asked, amused.

"Who knows?" Chiun said. "It appears to be a national pastime. Nevertheless. I will examine the patient."

He brushed by the tall doctor and moved to the bedside. The patient, a fiftyish man with a red tight skinned face, looked at him hopefully.

"What is the nature of your pain?" Chiun asked him.

The man put a hand on his lower abdomen. "Here," he said.

Chiun looked at the spot a moment. "Do you eat meat?" he asked.

"Meat? Sure."

"Do not eat meat any more. Except for duck. Eat rice and fish." Chiun nodded his head for emphasis.

The patient looked at him, then over Chiun's shoulder at the other doctor.

"If I cure you, will you promise?" Chiun asked.

"Sure. I promise."

"All right." Chiun pulled the cover over the man down, exposing his long scrawny legs. Chiun snaked his long-nailed fingers down along the man's left leg, feeling, probing. He reached to the top of the foot, squeezed a moment and nodded in satisfaction when the patient grimaced. He pressed his left index finger on that spot, and reached his right hand under the foot. Then he pressed his two fingers toward each other, the man's foot imprisoned between them.

"Ouch. That hurts," the man called.

"Silence," Chiun commanded. "I am curing you." He returned to his task, this time with greater pressure.

The patient bit his lip against the pain and then gasped as Chiun gave the foot a final twist between his fingers.

"There," he said. "It is done."

The doctor who had been watching this stepped forward. "Just what is done?"

"The patient's pain. It will soon be gone. His stomach will work. He will be well again. He will eat no more meat and therefore will not suffer this illness again."

The doctor looked at the patient, who looked at first stunned, then a slow smile spread over his face.

141

"Hey. The stomach. It doesn't hurt anymore."

"Of course not," Chiun said. "Obey my orders. No more meat."

The tall doctor moved to the patient and began to press into his stomach with his fingertips. "Does it hurt here? Here? Here?"

The patient shook his head. "I tell you, doc, it doesn't hurt anymore."

The doctor shrugged and turned to Chiun. "Doctor Park, you say?"

"Yes. Who else can we help?"

"Right this way."

As they moved through the hospital corridors, Chiun explained his background. He had studied medicine under the personal tutelage of that great doctor, Lance Ravenel.

"Lance Ravenel?"

Chiun nodded.

"I have never heard of him, I'm sorry to say."

"Do you not watch 'As the Planet Revolves' on the daytime television?"

"'As the Planet Revolves'? Dr. Ravenel?"

"Yes. The beautiful story is about him," Chiun said. "He is a very fine doctor."

Thus did the Master of Sinanju try to impart wisdom to a so-called physician in the United States of America. And he was repaid by this so-called physician who put hands upon him and did declare that he was taking him to the authorities. Whereupon, the Master of Sinanju did deposit this so-called physician in a broom closet. This, did the Master explain to Remo later in their room.

"I am disgusted with the state of American medicine, Remo," he said.

"Forget that? Did you kill the doctor?"

"Kill? I? Here in this institution to help the ailing? I only put him to sleep."

"Thank God for that. And then what happened?"

"I talked to other doctors. They were not interested in my plan."

"Which was?"

"I explained to them the truth that the people in this hospital were not sick, but were faking. I told them what they should do. Did they listen? No."

"What did you tell them to do?"

"Aha," Chiun said. "A brilliant plan. Take the six sickest persons. Execute them as a lesson to the others. That would show them that they must stop this faking."

"But they wouldn't listen," Remo said.

"Correct," Chiun responded. "They would prefer their pills and their knives. Anything rather than use their heads."

"Do not be upset, Little Father. The world is just not ready for your hospital-emptying plan."

"I am disgusted, Remo. They had not even heard of Dr. Ravenel. I am beginning to think that program must be devised in England. I understand they have very good medicine and doctors in England. I think I will tell these doctors they should go to England to become as good doctors as they have in England."

"You do that, Chiun," said Remo. "I'm sure they'll be delighted at your suggestion."

CHAPTER THIRTEEN

Remo decided to talk to Dr. Demmet, a decision which had been made somewhat earlier by Kathy Hahl.

She found Demmet in an X-ray laboratory where he was filling in for the radiologist, overseeing the work of an intern who was processing X-ray plates.

When he saw Kathy Hahl come through the door, all boobs and buttocks in a short white skirt, Demmet told the intern to take an early lunch. The intern grinned at Demmet after eyeing Kathy Hahl himself, and when the young doctor left, he conspicuously locked the door behind him.

"Insolent bastard," said Kathy Hahl, after the door closed.

"No worse than most. The doctors they're turning out today are shit," Demmet said. He sat behind a desk, looking at reports, and his voice was thick.

"Like a drink?" he said. Kathy Hahl shook her head. As he reached into a desk drawer and brought out a pint bottle of vodka, she moved alongside his desk and perched herself on the edge of a table at his left hand.

"Don't mind if I drink alone, do you?"

She shook her head. "You're doing a lot of that

these days," she said. Her voice was a soft, sexy, unmistakable scold.

"Why not? It's one of the things I do really well." He poured the liquor into a water tumbler and drank one-third of it at a gulp. Then he refilled the glass, capped the bottle and put it away.

"Still feeling sorry for yourself?" she asked. Slowly she raised her legs and propped them up on his open desk drawer, pulling her knees up close to her bosom. Her skirt fell loose from behind her thighs. "You used to be interested in more than self-pity," she said, invitingly.

"I used to be a lot of things," Demmet said, again sipping from the glass. "I used to be a pretty good doctor, you know."

"And you used to be a gambler who didn't pay his bookmaker and was going to wind up wearing cement boots on the bottom of the river. So don't give me that what-could-have-been crap," she said.

He drank again, then glumly said, "To what do I owe the honor?"

"We've got work to do."

"Oh?"

"Yes. That Williams who checked in. He's a fraud. He's been nosing around the hospital asking questions."

"So what?"

"He's been asking questions about you," she said. "I think he's a government man."

"Let him ask. What's he going to find out?"

"He's liable to find out that you were in attendance on every one of those IRS people who mysteriously died during minor operations. I don't know about you, but I'd rather he didn't find that out."

"Well, then, you stop him from finding out," Demmet said, emptying the glass and carefully setting it

145

down into a dark, wet, green ring on his desk blotter. "I'm finished killing people for you."

"This one's not for me. It's for you," Kathy Hahl said.

"No way," Demmet said. He took the bottle from the desk drawer again and Kathy Hahl withdrew her legs from the drawer and propped them up in front of her on the edge of the table. She ran her hands slowly down the backs of her white thighs and watched silently as Demmet poured himself a drink.

She shook her head slightly. It was bad enough that Demmet was becoming a drunk. But he was losing his nerve, and that could be fatal. Before she allowed it to be fatal for her, she would see to it that it was fatal for him.

Demmet drank sullenly from his glass, then turned to her.

He looked at her face and she smiled warmly at him. Then he let his eyes drop to the long curved legs, the milky white tautness of the thighs. She moved her hands farther around the backs of her legs until they met in front of her. She began to stroke herself, fingertip gentle, lovingly.

"It's been a long time, Dan," she said. Her smile was all snow white and invitation warm. "How about it?" she asked.

"I'd rather drink," he said.

"You think that, Dan. But remember. Remember how it is. Remember the tricks I do." He looked at her face and she touched the tip of her tongue to her partially opened lips. "Remember?" she said breathily.

"Remember the golf course? And the time down on the morgue table? And in my office? How many times in my office, Dan? A dozen? A hundred?"

She stood up and moved alongside him, slipping her hand inside his shirt and beginning to twist the hair

146

on his chest. She put her face close to his ear. "Remember?" she taunted.

Demmet drank from his glass. "I don't want to remember."

"But you can't forget, can you, Dan?" she said. Her hand slid from his chest down along his stomach. "Can you, Dan?" Despite himself, Demmet felt himself being aroused, his body awakening. She darted her tongue tip into his left ear. Demmet tried to concentrate on the glass of vodka in front of him. Her tongue wetted the inside of his ear and then he felt a suction on his ear as she glued her lips to it.

With a muffled roar, Demmet rose to his feet. He threw his arms around Kathy Hahl and buried his face in her neck.

"You bitch," he cried. "You great sex-fiend bitch."

His shoulders heaved. Kathy Hahl could feel them as her chin rested on his left shoulder. He was weeping. "Yes," she said. "I am a great sex-fiend bitch and I want a great sex-fiend man. You. Right now. Don't make me wait."

Her hands fumbled at his belt. She loosened it and Demmet felt his trousers begin to slide from him. He used his weight to force her back onto the empty gray-plastic-topped table. With his left hand he worked her skirt up around her hips. She wore nothing under her skirt.

He wanted to hurt her, to overpower her, to punish her with his sex. But when they were joined, he felt her body begin to quiver and the motion and the contact were too much for him and he felt himself losing control and the motion increased and then he was drifting, just drifting, through a world of exploding fireworks and loud noises, and he felt her fingertips pinching his bare buttocks, and it hurt, but exquisitely, and his pouring out was explosive and all

147

his being was concentrated in that, so much that he did not even feel, among the pinches, the pin prick as the needle-ring pressed into his left buttock and deposited its supply of fluid into his soft tissues.

He lay against Kathy Hahl, spent, quivering, disgusted with himself, and heard her laugh. "Not bad that time, Dan," she said. "I think you lasted about twelve seconds."

"You slut," he said, pushing back from her. "You evilminded slut."

"Oh, come on, Dan. Stop it. Have a drink and you'll feel better. If I remember, that's something you said you were good at."

"You slut," he said.

Kathy Hahl stood up and smoothed her garments. "If that's the way you feel," she said. "I'm leaving."

"I'm not going to touch Williams," Demmet said.

"I know that," Kathy Hahl said. "So let's just forget it. I'll do it myself." She turned and walked from the room, locking it again behind her.

Demmet watched her go, then sheepishly pulled up his trousers and buckled his belt. It was only when he sat back down at the desk that he felt the small twinge of pain in his left buttock. He reached under him with his hand and then realized in horror what probably had caused the pain. Disgust with what he had done turned to terror at what he feared Kathy Hahl had just done to him.

"Where's Doctor Demmet?" Remo asked.

"I don't know, sir. I'll check." She dialed three digits on her phone, and after a brief conversation hung up and told Remo:

"He's filling in for Dr. Walker today in radiology. He's in the X-ray office in Room 414."

"Thank you, nurse."

Outside Room 414, Remo saw a young red-haired man knocking loudly on the door.

"What's going on here?" asked Remo.

"I'm Doctor Royce. I'm working with Dr. Demmet today, I just came back from lunch and he doesn't answer my knocks on the door."

"Let me see that door," Remo said, moving in front of the intern. Shielded by his body, he drove his fingertips into the door next to the knob. The wood splintered, the metal of the lock broke loose at its pivot point, and the door swung open into the room.

"Just stuck," Remo said to the intern.

He stepped inside the room, the young doctor behind him, and looked around for Demmet. There was no sign of anyone there. Remo felt a cold breeze and looked off to the right. A window behind a string of filing cabinets was open. As he looked at it, Remo could see a flash of white fabric blowing in the wind outside the open window. The intern saw it too and ran toward it.

He peered outside. "Dr. Demmet," he cried. "What are you doing?"

"It's all right, kid," came a voice that Remo recognized as Demmet's. "It's all right. You did good work on those plates."

"Come in from there, sir," the intern yelled.

"Never again, kid. Never again."

The intern turned and looked at Remo with a helpless expression on his face. Remo looked around the room. There was another window to the left. He moved up onto the filing cabinets, opened the window and was through it.

A narrow two-inch stone ledge ran along the side of the building outside the fourth-floor window. Remo moved out onto it. He tensed his legs, forcing the thrust of his body inward against the wall, overcoming the incorrect distribution of weight that put most of his force downward, out, off the ledge, over open space. He looked up as he moved. Twenty feet away was the corner of the building. Demmet was ten feet around the corner to the right. One arm up against the wall, Remo moved crablike, foot past foot, turning the corner of the building, using his hand as a claw, turning the weight of his body in against the wall, moving steadily, for if he stopped his forward motion the force of gravity would hurl him down. He reached the corner of the building, twenty feet away, and used both hands while moving smoothly around the corner.

Demmet was in front of him, his heels on the ledge, his arms over his head, holding on to a porcelain electric insulator. Demmet saw him.

"What do you want?" Demmet said.

"Let's go inside and I'll tell you about it."

"Who are you?"

"Name's Williams," Remo said.

He kept moving toward Demmet, because to stop moving was to fall.

"I've heard about you," Demmet said thickly and Remo realized he was drunk. "I don't want to talk to you."

"Beats standing out here in the cold," Remo said.

"Cold? What cold?" Demmet asked. He giggled. The convulsions of his laughter shook his body. Remo could see his fingers start to slip from his overhead support. Demmet's hands dropped. He waved his arms for a moment as if trying to retain his balance on the two-inch-wide ledge and then he turned his face toward Remo in a look that was more of sorrow than of fright.

"I don't want to grow old," he said. The last word was drawn out long and loud as the air was pulled from his lungs, for Demmet had lost his balance and was falling forward, down toward the parking lot four stories below. He landed on top of a Fleetwood Brougham with a clapping smack. Remo meanwhile kept moving along the wall and then darted in through the window Demmet had opened.

The intern stood there, shock on his face.

"Sorry, kid," Remo said. "I tried."

The intern nodded numbly and walked past Remo, looking out over the file cabinets and peering down at Demmet's body, sprawled motionless on top of the car in the lot.

The intern swallowed, then looked to his left. For the first time, he noticed the ledge on which Demmet had precariously perched his heels. Only two inches wide. How had that doctor . . . what was his name, Williams? . . . been able to move along that to try to get to Demmet?

He turned back to the room. "How did you . . ." But the room was empty. Remo had gone.

CHAPTER FOURTEEN

The story of Remo's miraculous walk along the two-inch ledge outside Robler Clinic's fourth floor would surely have been all over the hospital if the first person the intern had told had not been Kathy Hahl.

But Ms. Hahl, the hospital's assistant administrator, had carefully explained to the young intern how important it was that Mr. Williams not be mentioned. How he was planning to make a substantial gift to the hospital's research program, a gift that might very well create a large number of special openings for bright young doctors, but that the gift would be lost if there were publicity.

"After all," she explained, putting her arm around the young man warmly and impressing her breasts against his upper arm, "he really didn't have anything to do with Dr. Demmet's tragic death. I mean, he just tried to save him but couldn't. There's no reason for publicity about that."

The intern impressed equally by her logic and the free feel, agreed.

"I think that's the best course of action," she said. "Why don't you come by my office late tomorrow and we'll discuss it some more?" she said, openly inviting.

Flustered, the young intern agreed and left. When

the door closed behind him, Kathy Hahl went back behind her desk to think.

Whatever he was supposed to be, this Mr. Williams was not. He was certainly not some recluse billionaire trying to hide out in a hospital. He was certainly not trying to find a way to escape IRS trouble.

He was a government agent. Of that there was no longer any doubt. He had proved that with his stupid heavy-handed hint and his clumsy snooping around the laboratory.

He was probably dumb, but he was also dangerous. The impossible walk on that unpassable ledge had shown that. Kathy Hahl went to her window, opened it wide and looked at the ledge. Two inches wide. It seemed impossible, or so she had thought when the intern first told her the story. But the young doctor, while nervous, was not hysterical and not in shock. He was simply reporting a fact and Kathy Hahl, who had gone to Demmet's office to make sure that Demmet had not left a note implicating her, was the first person he had spoken to.

The walk was impossible . . . and yet he had done it. Williams must be quite a man.

At the thought, she smiled slightly to herself.

The operative word was "man." He was a man for all his talent. And she had ways to deal with men.

Dr. Smith, at CURE's Folcroft headquarters in Rye, New York, had already heard of Demmet's death when he talked to Remo that afternoon.

"You responsible for that?" he asked.

"No, dammit," Remo said. "He was my chief suspect."

"So?"

"So now I don't know. Just before he fell, he said something strange about not wanting to get old. It kind of reminded me of Stace and Mrs. Wilberforce."

"I received autopsy reports on Stace and Mrs. Wilberforce," Smith said.

"And?"

"The reports showed extreme aging. Senility. General breakdown of body tissues and bodily function, usually associated with very advanced age. Yet Stace was fifty-five and Mrs. Wilberforce sixty-two."

"Any ideas?" Remo asked.

"None. The computer reports no known chemical agent that can produce that kind of effect."

"I think there is," Remo said. "There's an experimental lab here and I've seen some old-looking animals in it."

"Well, stay with it," Smith said.

"Right. I'm going to sit here and figure it out. No violence."

"Good. No more Scrantons. Don't hesitate to use Chiun, by the way."

"Use Chiun? What do you mean?"

"Well, he seems to be rather good at thinking things through. Use his brain if you need it."

"Are you implying that I'm not smart enough to figure this out myself?"

"Something like that," Smith said agreeably.

"Well, for your information, Smitty, your so-called Korean genius is out right now looking in this hospital for Marcus Welby. How about that?"

"Chiun will probably find him. Use him."

"Right." Remo hung up. It was annoying, having decided to use brains after being chewed out for using muscle, to have Upstairs imply that you weren't any good for using anything but muscle. It was the $25,000 that had put Smith in a snit. Smith guarded CURE's money as if it were his own and Remo's demand for $25,000 to impress the hospital staff and to guarantee his freedom and his privacy had stuck in Smith's throat like an unpeeled grapefruit.

"Bitch, bitch, bitch," Remo said to himself as he lay back on the bed. The door pushed open and he looked toward it, expecting to see Chiun, but the tall bosomy redhead he had seen at Mrs. Wilberforce's bedside walked in instead.

"Mr. Williams," she said, "remember me? I'm Kathy Hahl, the assistant administrator."

"Sure," said Remo.. "Nice place you've got here."

"Thank you, we like it. I just stopped into see if there's anything you'd like." She moved closer to Remo's couch and looked down at him, eyes flashing.

"Not unless you have a doctor on your staff named Marcus Welby. Or a spare singer named Barbra Streisand." To her blank look, he said, "No? Then I guess I don't need anything."

"I had something more concrete in mind."

"Such as."

"Such as a tour of the hospital. I understand you've been looking it over yourself."

"Yes, a little."

"I heard of your attempt to save Dr. Demmet today. It was very brave."

"Not really," Remo said. "Anybody would have done the same thing."

She leaned forward over his couch, her breasts jutting out almost over him. "You're a very strange man," she said. "I don't mind telling you that when *I* heard you were coming I thought you'd be a crotchety old man. I never expected you."

"An improvement?" asked Remo, eyeing her breasts because she seemed to want him to and he didn't want to disappoint her. Besides, they were very nice breasts.

"A decided improvement. So would you really like

to see our research facilities? We're into some exciting work."

Remo smiled and rose from the couch, brushing against her as he got up. He slipped on his gumsoled shoes and Kathy Hahl looked down at his feet. "Are those your only shoes?"

He nodded. "Why?"

"They cause static electricity. And there are too many flammables up there. The staff would go ape if they saw you there with those on. Tell you what. Wait here and I'll get some safe shoes for you."

Remo fell back onto the couch. "I'll wait."

"It'll be worth the wait," she said, leaving the room.

He watched her trim buttocks swish away. At time like that, he really understood how shameful it was that Chiun had robbed him of the pleasure of sex. Sex was just another discipline, another skill to be learned. Remo had learned it, and now he had trouble staying awake. He probably could fall asleep during the act if it weren't for the noises of passion generally made by his partners. Looking at Kathy Hahl, he decided it was a double shame now because in a different time, place and setting, he would have liked to meet Ms. Hahl.

Remo was remembering long-ago pleasures when two men walked into his room pushing a wheelchair. It was the black-haired Freddy, and the blond-haired Al, whom he had met in the lab that morning. If they recognized him without his doctor's gown and black sunglasses, they gave no indication.

"Mr. Williams?" the dark-haired one asked.

Behind him, Remo saw the blond man lock the door to the room.

"Yeah."

"We couldn't find any shoes in your size, so Ms. Hahl said to bring you up in the wheelchair."

Remo got to his feet and strolled toward the chair, trying not to laugh aloud at the clumsy trap. How stupid did they think he was?

"How come you couldn't find any shoes in my size when you didn't know what my size was?"

"Errrr. Actually, we didn't have no shoes at all anymore. So hop in here and we'll take you up."

"Sure thing," said Remo, cheerily, wondering what they were up to.

He plopped into the wheelchair. "Hey, I never rode in one of these things before. Can I turn the wheels?"

"As much as you want," said the dark-haired man, moving around behind him. "He sure can, can't he, Al?"

The blond man at the door chuckled. "Sure. Anything he wants."

Remo sat back in the chair, put his arms on the arm rests, and closed his eyes. "Home, James," he said.

"You're home," the man behind him said. "Wise guy."

Remo had been careless. He hadn't paid attention and now he felt a needle jam into the muscles of his shoulder. Dammit, he thought. It might be poison. What a stupid thing to do. Suddenly his head began to hurt.

"Biggest dose yet," said the blond man at the door.

Remo's head was splitting. He tried to rise, but felt something brush against his face, something made of cloth. Then he felt his hands being raised. His arms were jammed into sleeves. He felt his arms being drawn around his body and they seemed to be locked into place. It was a . . . a something . . . what was it? A straitjacket. They had put him into a straitjacket.

The two men hoisted him to his feet. If only his head would stop hurting. "What is that stuff?" he said thickly.

"You're not old enough to know about that," one of the men said. "Yet," he added with a chuckle.

Remo felt himself thrown roughly onto the sofa and then heard the rubber-tired wheelchair squeak as it was moved from the room. He heard the door lock shut behind the two men. His head felt as if it had ballooned to twice its normal size. The pain behind his eyes was racking. His mouth was dry and he felt a chill shudder his body.

He had to get out. The locked door would stop anyone from looking in on him. He was lying on his stomach, his arms crisscrossed in front of his body, pinned down by his own weight.

He strained to roll over onto his back. Each movement brought a new hammer of pain to his head. The hurt was spreading now from behind his eyes into the center of his skull, into the brain.

What had they dosed him with? The aging drug. But what could he do about it?

Exhausted, he was on his back. He lay there momentarily, hoping to regain his strength, but he could feel his strength draining away as if it were water flowing out an open faucet.

He could not wait. He tried to ignore the pain, to reach deep into his essence for new strength, but the pain was overpowering. Remo sighed and made one last effort to draw on whatever reserves he might still have. He managed to turn his right hand over, so that the fingers were facing upward, away from his body, toward the ceiling. Against his curled fingertips he felt the rough coarse threads of the straitjacket. No room to move. No way to do it. No. Keep trying. He pulled his right hand back, pressing it hard againt his left hip, buying a half-inch of room inside the sleeve of the jacket. With all the force he could rouse, he drove his fingertips upward against the material of the jacket.

Doctor Shiva. Ms. Hahl said you'd tell me about the aging drug."

"Oh, you know. Well, I'm very happy to meet you." The woman stood up and came toward Remo. "I'm Dr. Hildie. I developed the drug, you know."

"How does it work?"

The woman walked by Remo out into the laboratory. She picked up a stoppered test tube half-filled with a clear heavy oily liquid.

"This is it," she said. "And these are some of the results of our work," she added, waving toward the animal cages. For the first time since he'd entered, Remo heard the animal chatter.

"Yes, I know," he said. "Freddy and Al showed me the other day. But how does the drug work?"

"If you remember, Doctor Shiva, about a year ago, some scientists discovered an unidentified protein in the bodies of the elderly. That protein was not to be found in the bodies of the young. It occurred to me that if aging produced this protein, perhaps the protein could produce aging. We were able here, with Ms. Hahl's help and funding, to make the protein synthetically and greatly intensify its strength."

"And it's worked?"

"It certainly has, as these animals show."

"What about human experiments?"

"Oh, no," she said. "We've never had any of those. And what would be the purpose anyway? There's value in learning how to bring animals to maturity more rapidly, but not humans. Oh, no."

"How is the protein given?" Remo asked. "By injection?"

She nodded. "First we tried it in food, but that was too slow. The best way is to inject it into the bloodstream. The absorption rate of the fluid," she said, holding up the test tube, "is very great. It can be absorbed by any soft body tissues. Injection is fastest."

"But if I rubbed it, say, on my arm, it would work?"

"Yes," she said, "though the tough skin covering off the arm would slow down its effects. But, for instance, your tongue would absorb it much more rapidly. Any soft, open tissue."

"I see," Remo said. "Well, thank you, Doctor Hildie. You don't mind if I look around for myself, do you?"

"Of course not. I'll be inside if you need me."

"Wonderful. I'll call you."

Doctor Hildie returned the test tube to its holder and walked back toward her office. Poor thing knew nothing, Remo thought, and had no idea how her great discovery was being used. He waited until she was out of sight, in her office, before he picked up the test tube carefully and stuck it into the chest pocket of his shirt.

Then he headed back toward the door. Kathy Hahl's office was down the corridor to the left.

They were so surprised to see the back of an old man, sitting on the floor watching television, that Freddy and Al failed to notice the torn straitjacket on the couch when they entered Remo's suite.

"Williams?" said Freddy.

Chiun turned slowly, his leathered face lit in blue from the flickering light of the TV tube.

Freddy, the dark-haired one, looked at him and giggled. "I knew there was something wrong with Williams. The eyes were a giveaway. He's part Chink."

Chiun looked at them, still saying nothing.

Al shook his blond hair from his eyes. "It's eerie," he said. "Look at him. Only about a half hour, it took."

"How do you feel, Williams?" asked Freddy. "Headache go yet? Do you know what you look like? Like Confucius. You're ancient. But don't worry, man. Not

166

much longer. Pretty soon, different parts of you aren't going to work any more and pretty soon after that, you'll be dead." He giggled again. "Sound like fun?"

"You two imbeciles were the deliverers of the poison?" Chiun asked. But it wasn't really a question, more a statement of fact.

"See? Your memory's already starting to go. You don't remember us, do you?" Freddy said.

"No," Chiun said. "But you will remember me in the few moments you have yet to live."

Freddy and Al moved into the room.

"Oh, you frighten me to pieces . . . old man," Freddy snapped sarcastically. "Doesn't he frighten you terribly, Al?"

"Oh, heavens to Betsy, yes. I'm pissing my pants."

"It is the way with untrained babies. And beasts," Chiun said.

"Hey, hey, hey. Pretty chipper," Al said.

Chiun ignored him. "Because you are going to die, I am going to tell you the reason."

"Oh, yes," Freddy mocked. "Tell us the reason, before you tear us apart with your bare hands." He winked at Al.

"You are going to die because you laid a hand upon the child of the Master of Sinanju."

Al rotated his finger near his temple. "He's gone, Freddy. Maybe the big dose wipes out the brain. Nutty as a fruitcake."

Freddy said, "We'd better put him back in the jacket, so he doesn't create any row. How'd you get out of that anyway, Williams?"

Chiun rose slowly to his feet, twisting as he rose so he faced the two men across five feet of carpeting.

He was silent.

"Well, it doesn't matter," Freddy said. "Let's get

167

you back into it." He walked forward, extending his arms to put them on Chiun's shoulders.

His fingertips were only inches from Chiun's shoulders when there was a yellow blur as Chiun's hand moved. Freddy felt the side of his neck turn wet. He clapped his hand to his head and felt, under his palm, that his right ear had been severed.

"Bastard," he shouted and turned at Chiun, swinging a roundhouse right hand. But it hit nothing and again Freddy felt the pain, but this time on the left side of his head. His other ear was gone and the blood ran wildly down the side of his jaw and neck.

Chiun stood motionless as if rooted in the one spot.

Freddy screamed, his hands over the gaping wounds where his ears had been. Al stepped forward to help him, but before he could intercede, he saw two long-nailed hands flash out and he heard the crack as they hit into Freddy's head. It was a sickening, breaking sound; Freddy dropped to the floor and Al knew he was dead.

Al stopped halfway in his charge, then turned and fled toward the door. But alongside him—by God, the old man was moving along the wall—there was a green figure, and then the grim aged Oriental specter stood in front of the door, a hand upraised to stop him.

Al swallowed, then charged, and Chiun imposed upon him a slow lingering death, before he experienced which, Al wet his pants.

Chiun stepped over the bodies and went back to the television set which was now booming organ music and showing the introductions to his personal rerun of that day's showing of "As the Planet Revolves." Chiun looked around at the corpses, the blood, the vomit, the various body parts, and shook his head sadly. Remo would have to clean up this mess. The room was getting disgusting.

CHAPTER SIXTEEN

Kathy Hahl was bent over a file cabinet, sticking papers into a briefcase, when Remo went into her office. He moved silently toward her, reached around her and grasped her breasts.

He squeezed them gently, his fingers kneading the tips through her thin sweater. He could feel her instant arousal, and he pressed his lower body against hers.

"Don't stop," she said. "Keep going."

"Is that any way to talk to a man who's going to be old enough to be your grandfather?"

He released her, stepped back, and she turned around. Her face showed her shock at seeing him, then she relaxed into a smile.

"I'm surprised to see you still up and about," she said, "Mr. Williams. Is it really Mr. Williams?"

"Yes, it is. Remo Williams."

"Are you really a billionaire hermit?"

"Afraid not. Just your everyday garden-variety assassin."

"I see," she said. "How do you feel? Has the headache gone yet?"

"I just got over it."

"That's normal. The aging process starts any moment now. You may already be able to feel it. Does the skin at the side of your eyes start to feel a little tight? That's the loss of elasticity that comes with age. And the back of your hands. Your veins should become more pronounced and the skin should start to wrinkle. Has that happened yet? No worry. Any moment now."

"Good. It'll give me something to look forward to," Remo said.

"How did you get here? Freddy and Al went down for you."

"They missed me. I'm sure they found enough to keep them busy."

"Remo Williams, eh? Who are you with? The IRS? The FBI?"

"None of those. I'm kind of a freelance for the government. Tell me, Kathy, since it doesn't matter any more, what was this all about? Was it just the money?"

She smiled, showing even, crystal white teeth. "Since it doesn't matter, I'll tell you. Sure it was the money. But not the small change I got for doing in people on the table."

"And the big money?"

"This hospital is used by two dozen of the top officials in the federal government for annual checkups, routine medical treatment, that kind of thing. Can you imagine what other governments would pay to have me produce instant old age in, say, the secretary of state? Maybe on the eve of a big summit conference?"

"Kathy, that's downright unpatriotic," said Remo.

"Sure, but highly productive. And I was just about to begin. I figured Mrs. Wilberforce for our last guinea pig. And then you came here, and got a little too close for comfort. Why did you come up here, by the way? I hate to see people die."

"I came up because I thought since I was going to leave the world anyway, I'd do it with a bang, not a whimper."

She smiled. "You can try. But I do this thing to men. Ten seconds is all they can take."

"I should have that much time left," said Remo.

He scooped her up in his arms and bore her back toward the filing cabinet where he placed her down gently.

"I think the position we started in would be satisfactory," he said.

"Far be it from me to stifle an old man's fantasy," she said. She turned away, over the open file drawer, and smiled to herself. The drug was working of course. And the longer she kept him here, the surer would be the result. Maybe she'd let him prolong it. She'd give him, perhaps, a full thirty seconds of ecstasy. She felt her skirt being lifted up around her hips, and then she felt Remo. He felt strangely oily, but the lubrication was somehow exciting. Maybe forty seconds, she thought.

Then it was underway, but he was like no one else had ever been. His body was strong and with his hands he controlled her movements. She counted to fifteen and then began an internal movement which men had always told her they had never experienced before, but he matched it with a movement and a swelling of his own, and she kept counting but when she reached thirty, she stopped, because she was too busy moaning her pleasure. There was pleasure again, and again, and again, and through it all, she wished that she did not really have to kill this Remo, because after all these years, she had found a man whose performance matched her appetites. And there was pleasure again and again.

How long it went on, she did not know, but then,

without reaching his own peak, he was gone, moving away from her.

She hung there, over the file cabinet, trying to catch her breath. She heaved a big sigh and turned. He was zipped up and in his fingers he was holding a test tube from the laboratory. She recognized it. He dropped it into her wastepaper basket.

"Empty," he said. "No point in saving an empty container."

"Was that . . ." she said, pointing.

"Right," he said. "Your aging oil. You know, if it doesn't work the way you wanted it, you could always package it as a sex lubricant."

"But why?" she said.

"Tissues, honey. Absorption. Right now, that juice should be pouring through your bloodstream. You'd better sit down. You don't look any too well."

Remo pulled her roughly toward her desk and lowered her into her seat.

"And you? It's on your tissues, too, you know," she said.

"Sorry, sweetheart. I'm immune."

She put her hands out in front of her on the desk, then clapped them to her head as the pain exploded behind her eyes, inside her temples. It was a blinding flash, and then gone.

"The pain'll get worse before it gets better," Remo said. He took her hands from her head and extended them before her on the desk. "It's a shame," he said. "Look at these hands. A young woman like you with such old woman's hands. You should change your detergent."

As she looked down at her hands, she saw that indeed they were harder looking, dry, almost wrinkled. Before her eyes, she saw in horror small veins on the backs of her hands begin to swell and rise under the skin. She was aging. Growing old. Right at her desk, before her own eyes.

She looked up at Remo with hopeless panic on her face.

He shrugged. "That's the biz, sweetheart," he said, and then left, jamming the door on his way out. It would be hours before anybody could get in. By that time, Kathy Hahl would be out of it. For good.

He felt fine as he walked down the hall toward the corridor to his room.

He whistled "Deck the Halls."

CHAPTER SEVENTEEN

"For crying out loud, Chiun, what's Smith going to say?"

Chiun sat impassively, watching his television set.

"Don't pull that do-not-disturb business with me," Remo said. "I know you're watching reruns. Just look at this place. Ears on the floor for crying out loud. Bodies, vomit, blood. Don't you ever clean up?"

Chiun listened only to Dr. Lance Ravenel.

"And you know Smith didn't want any violence. No more Scrantons. And now you've run amok. What's wrong with you anyway? If you don't have any Christmas spirit, at least you could be good-humored for the Feast of the Pig."

Dr. Ravenel was talking to Mrs. Claire Wentworth in his office at Brookfield Hospital, about the prognosis for her daughter who was suffering an overdose of Quaalude.

"I think we'll have good news for you tomorrow," Dr. Ravenel said.

On the television screen, the distinguished looking actor rose and came alongside Mrs. Wentworth, whom he had loved twenty years before, back before her marriage to old Josiah Wentworth, the clothing tycoon.

"Yes," Dr. Ravenel said. "I think we'll have a fine

Christmas present for you. I think our daughter's going to be all right," he said, exposing to anyone retarded enough not to have guessed it six years earlier, that Mrs. Wentworth's daughter had been fathered by him.

Ravenel put his arm around her. The camera panned back. Dr. Ravenel and Mrs. Wentworth stood silhouetted against a giant Christmas tree.

"A merry Christmas," Mrs. Wentworth said.

"A very merry Christmas," Dr. Ravenel said.

"Your tree is beautiful," Mrs. Wentworth said.

"Yes, it is. The most beautiful Christmas tree I've even seen," said Dr. Ravenel.

"Aaaiieee," said Chiun, reaching forward and slapping off the television set.

He rose. Remo said nothing.

Chiun turned.

"One can trust nothing in this country. Nothing. Those doctors turn out to be fakers. And people in whose judgment you trust turn out to have no taste. Why did he like that tree?"

"It was a beautiful tree, Chiun."

"No. What I gave you was a beautiful tree. Even if it was not appreciated. You are not going to give me the gift I sought?"

Remo shook his head. "I can't."

"All right. In its place, you may clean up this mess."

Remo shook his head.

It was therefore agreed upon by a mutual silence of thirty seconds that they would leave the debris in the room for the sweeper and Smith and his reactions be damned.

They rode the elevator down in silence. In the lobby at the desk was the same guard who had greeted them upon their arrival.

175

Chiun motioned to Remo to wait and walked to the guard.

"Do you remember me?" he asked.

The guard looked puzzled, then his face brightened. "Sure. Doctor Park, wasn't it?"

"Yes. Tell me, have you looked at this tree?" Chiun asked, waving over his shoulder at the huge fire behind him.

The guard said, "Funny, I never did until you mentioned it. But now I look at it all the time. It's beautiful." He stood up, reached forward and took Chiun's hand. "I wanted to thank you for helping me to see it. It was really clever, how you did it. Thank you, Doctor Park. And a merry Christmas."

Chiun just looked at him, then walked back to Remo.

"It is no wonder he is a hospital guard," he said. "He has taken leave of his senses."

They stepped out into the crisp December cold, Remo going first.

He was halfway down the steps when Chiun halted him.

"Remo," he called.

Remo turned slowly and looked back at Chiun who waited on the top step.

"Merry Christmas," Chiun said.

"Thank you," said Remo, meaning it.

"Even if you do not give me a gift."

The Destroyer by Warren Murphy

Remo Williams is the perfect weapon—a cold, calculating death machine developed by CURE, the world's most secret crime-fighting organization. Together with his mentor, Chiun, the oriental martial arts wizard, The Destroyer makes the impossible missions possible.

Over 13 million copies sold!

☐	40-235-X	Created, The Destroyer	#1	$1.50
☐	40-276-7	Death Check	#2	1.50
☐	40-277-5	Chinese Puzzle	#3	1.50
☐	40-278-3	Mafia Fix	#4	1.50
☐	40-279-1	Dr. Quake	#5	1.50
☐	40-280-5	Death Therapy	#6	1.50
☐	40-281-3	Union Bust	#7	1.50
☐	40-282-1	Summit Chase	#8	1.50
☐	40-283-X	Murder's Shield	#9	1.50
☐	40-284-8	Terror Squad	#10	1.50
☐	40-285-6	Kill or Cure	#11	1.50
☐	40-286-4	Slave Safari	#12	1.50
☐	40-287-2	Acid Rock	#13	1.50
☐	40-288-0	Judgment Day	#14	1.50
☐	40-289-9	Murder Ward	#15	1.50
☐	40-290-2	Oil Slick	#16	1.50
☐	40-291-0	Last War Dance	#17	1.50
☐	40-292-9	Funny Money	#18	1.50
☐	40-293-7	Holy Terror	#19	1.50
☐	40-294-5	Assassins Play-Off	#20	1.50
☐	40-295-3	Deadly Seeds	#21	1.50
☐	40-296-1	Brain Drain	#22	1.50
☐	40-297-X	Child's Play	#23	1.50
☐	40-298-8	King's Curse	#24	1.50
☐	40-236-8	Sweet Dreams	#25	1.50
☐	40-251-1	In Enemy Hands	#26	1.50
☐	40-353-4	Last Temple	#27	1.50
☐	40-416-6	Ship of Death	#28	1.50
☐	40-342-9	Final Death	#29	1.50
☐	40-110-8	Mugger Blood	#30	1.50
☐	40-153-1	Head Man	#31	1.50
☐	40-154-X	Killer Chromosomes	#32	1.50
☐	40-155-8	Voodoo Die	#33	1.50
☐	40-156-6	Chained Reaction	#34	1.50
☐	40-157-4	Last Call	#35	1.50
☐	40-158-2	Power Play	#36	1.50

the EXECUTIONER by Don Pendleton

Over 22 million copies in print!

DEATH MERCHANT

by Joseph Rosenberger

Over 3 million copies in print!

☐	40-483-2	Death Merchant	#1	$1.50
☐	40-417-4	Operation Overkill	#2	1.50
☐	40-458-1	Psychotron Plot	#3	1.50
☐	40-418-2	Chinese Conspiracy	#4	1.50
☐	40-419-0	Satan Strike	#5	1.50
☐	40-459-X	Albanian Connection	#6	1.50
☐	40-420-4	The Castro File	#7	1.50
☐	40-421-2	Billionaire Mission	#8	1.50
☐	220594-6	Laser War	#9	1.25
☐	220473-3	Mainline Plot	#10	1.25
☐	220561-5	Manhattan Wipeout	#11	1.25
☐	220642-3	KGB Frame	#12	1.25
☐	40-497-2	Mato Grosso Horror	#13	1.50
☐	220796-7	Vengeance: Golden Hawk	#14	1.25
☐	220823-9	Iron Swastika Plot	#15	1.25
☐	220857-7	Invasion of Clones	#16	1.25
☐	220880-9	Zemlya Expedition	#17	1.25
☐	220911-2	Nightmare in Algeria	#18	1.25
☐	40-460-3	Armageddon, USA!	#19	1.50
☐	40-256-2	Hell in Hindu Land	#20	1.50
☐	40-019-6	Pole Star Secret	#21	1.25
☐	40-043-6	Kondrashev Chase	#22	1.25
☐	40-078-5	Budapest Action	#23	1.25
☐	40-352-6	Kronos Plot	#24	1.50
☐	40-117-8	Enigma Project	#25	1.25
☐	40-118-3	Mexican Hit	#26	1.50
☐	40-119-1	Surinam Affair	#27	1.50
☐	40-254-6	Nipponese Nightmare	#28	1.50
☐	40-272-4	Fatal Formula	#29	1.50
☐	40-385-2	Shambhala Strike	#30	1.50
☐	40-392-5	Operation Thunderbolt	#31	1.50
☐	40-475-1	Deadly Manhunt	#32	1.50
☐	40-476-X	Alaska Conspiracy	#33	1.50

RICHARD BLADE

by Jeffrey Lord

Richard Blade is Everyman, a mighty and intrepid hero exploring the hitherto-uncharted realm of worlds beyond our knowledge, in the best tradition of America's most popular heroic fantasy giants such as Tarzan, Doc Savage, and Conan.

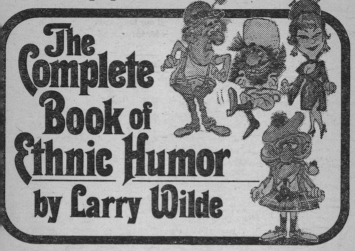

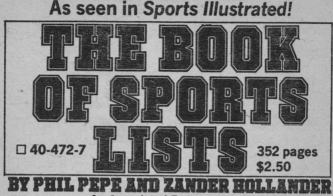